SHERLOCK HOLMES AND THE CROSBY MURDERS

The glamorous actress Susan Copely is being persecuted — and the reason lies in the events surrounding the wreck of the *Sophy Anderson* two decades before ... A well-regarded businessman appears to have brutally stabbed his wife to death, and then suffocated their two small children before fleeing their home. But Holmes, deploying his unique investigative methods, is set upon proving otherwise ... Finally, a most singular narrative from Mycroft Holmes at last sheds light upon what truly happened at the Reichenbach Falls that fateful day in 1891 ...

GARY LOVISI

✦

SHERLOCK HOLMES AND THE CROSBY MURDERS

Complete and Unabridged

LINFORD
Leicester

First published in Great Britain

First Linford Edition
published 2009

British Library CIP Data

Lovisi, Gary.
    Sherlock Holmes and the Crosby murders- -
(Linford mystery library)
    1. Holmes, Sherlock (Fictitious character)- -Fiction.
    2. Holmes, Mycroft (Fictitious character)- -Fiction.
    3. Murder- -Investigation- -Fiction.
    4. Detective and mystery stories.
    5. Large type books.
    I. Title II. Series
    823.9′14–dc22

    ISBN 978–1–84782–713–5

Published by
F. A. Thorpe (Publishing)
Anstey, Leicestershire

Set by Words & Graphics Ltd.
Anstey, Leicestershire
Printed and bound in Great Britain by
T. J. International Ltd., Padstow, Cornwall

This book is printed on acid-free paper

THE LOSS OF THE
SOPHY ANDERSON

1

The Actress

When overlooking my notes for the year 1887, I find that there is one case that stands out from all the others for the amount of danger in which it placed Sherlock Holmes and myself — not to mention the beautiful stage actress Susan Copely. It was a most ghastly affair and even now as I write these words, I shall leave them unpublished until after my death, for I could not inflict such a diabolical and tragic tale upon the reading public during my own lifetime.

I remember it all so vividly now. She was not unlike another famed actress, 'The Woman', as Holmes is fond of remembering Irene Adler in these later days. My publication of the Adler Case, which was Holmes' and my first case together, I had titled 'A Study in Scarlet'. It was still yet to appear on the magazine stalls in the *Beeton's Christmas Annual*. So it was with Irene Adler very much in my mind, that I prepared to write the far darker and disturbing account of what occurred in the case of the charming and graceful, Miss Susan Copely.

* * *

It was a cold night and quite late. Mrs. Hudson our indomitable housekeeper had retired many hours before, so it was I who answered the downstairs bell.

There, framed in the doorway to our flat I beheld a marvellous-looking woman. She was in her late twenties, beautiful of face and form, standing with that calm dignity you find in the most noble of royal ladies.

'May I come in, Doctor Watson?' she asked with a smile, for she could see that I was staring in wonder and delight, and too late my embarrassment had shown through. With some confusion I let her in and led her up the stairs to the rooms that Holmes and I inhabited.

'How is it that you know my name,

Madam?' I asked curiously.

'It is obvious. You can be none other than Doctor Watson,' she replied to my astonishment. The hint of a smile across her full lips showed that I had somehow amused her. She had obviously noticed my discomfiture and curiosity for she added in a little voice, 'Your every gesture speaks to me of the dedicated medical man, and there is other evidence to substantiate my hypothesis.'

'Really? Well, I would very much like to hear it,' I said eagerly, for I was sure that I had never met her before; nor did I think her any acquaintance of my companion.

We passed through the door to our flat and I turned awaiting some sort of answer. What I received was quite unexpected.

'You worked today in hospital, though that is quite not the usual for you,' she said. It was a statement, not a question. Then she added, 'It was Saint Barts, was it not?'

'Yes,' I replied carefully, though inwardly astonished. 'But how do you know?'

She smiled slightly again with a pixie

sort of grin. She was a real charmer all right, and in spite of knowing that fact, I could not help but like her all the more.

It was then that Sherlock Holmes entered the room. Immediately he and our visitor looked over each other appraisingly. I could feel the very air supercharged as if by electricity. It was a meeting of two extraordinary people of great will power and intellectual resources.

'My dear Mr. Holmes, it is so good to finally meet you,' our visitor said with genuine affection as her eyes shone on my companion. And I could see by his expression that her charm and beauty were already working their magic upon my friend.

Holmes came toward her and bowing expansively took her proffered hand kissing it with a gallantry I had rarely seen him evidence. 'And it is good to finally meet you, Lady Copely.'

'Please, Mr. Holmes, just plain Susan will do.'

'Of course,' Holmes replied with a smile. He seated himself in his favorite chair, opposite the one in which our guest was now seated.

'Well, I don't understand,' I began. 'I would like to know what is going on here. And how do you know I had done work at Saint Barts Hospital?'

'It was rushed work, was it not? You were in a great hurry to finish and get home by all accounts also,' Lady Copely added with a smile.

'Great God, Holmes! She is almost as annoying as you are sometimes.' I thought only Sherlock Holmes had this great power of deductive reasoning. It was most disconcerting for me, I can tell you, to discover another who apparently was Holmes' equal.

Both Holmes and Miss Copely laughed good-naturedly.

'I see you have met my long-suffering friend, Doctor John H. Watson, Susan,' Holmes said as he lit his pipe. Within a few seconds there were familiar smoke swirls slowly gliding all about the room.

'I am sorry if I unnerved you, Doctor, and I hope that you don't think too badly of me,' Susan said.

I had to smile at that. 'Of course not, it's just that your observations took me somewhat by surprise.'

'Then I will explain, if Mr. Holmes does not mind?'

'Pray continue, by all means. I shall find this bit of deduction most enlightening.' Holmes added as he puffed delightedly upon his pipe.

'It is obvious that you worked in a hospital today because you have a spot of blood upon the end of your right coat sleeve. As you are a well-dressed man, and hence obviously not the type of man who is in the habit of working while wearing his best clothes, it seems possible you were called away on some urgent business. What more urgent business could call a doctor than a medical emergency, a hospital emergency, no doubt. Am I right so far?'

I confessed that she was. Early that afternoon I had received a runner from Saint Barts concerning a patient of mine. It was a serious case, a friend who had asked to see me before the operation that would determine if he would live or die. I looked toward Susan and Holmes, 'I stayed with Mr. Withers until the surgeons came for him, and then was called upon to help out with an emergency case that had just been admitted. It was a terrible crime, a young man had been robbed and stabbed. He came stumbling into the hospital nearly dead with the loss of blood.' I replied, looking at her carefully. 'But how did you know it was Saint Barts Hospital?'

'It is obvious by the flecks of white dust that are upon your shoes and cuffs. The old Sanderson Warehouse is being demolished this week. It lies across the street from the hospital, now just an empty lot on which the hospital plans to expand. You were in a hurry, and took a short cut through that lot. If you were going to a hospital, it could only be Saint Barts because that is where the construction work is going on. You were also in such a rush to return to Baker Street that you did not allow yourself the time you normally would have to clean your trouser legs and shoes.'

I sat down astounded at this female counterpart to my detective friend. 'Why, it's amazing, Holmes!'

'Elementary, Watson!' he replied with a grin. I could see that he was pleased with our visitor. 'You have done extremely well, Susan.'

'Coming from you, Mr. Holmes, that is indeed a compliment.'

'But now you must tell Watson and myself what has brought you to our humble door and what it is that we may do for you?' Holmes added.

Susan Copely inhaled deeply and looked at Holmes with fear etched in her eyes. Whatever her strange story was, it had quite evidently unnerved her.

'I fear, Mr. Holmes, that I am in the gravest of danger. My life is in peril, and I am sure that because of our meeting, your life, and that of Doctor Watson are also in deadly peril.'

'That is quite all right, my dear. We have been in danger before, eh, Holmes?' I added confidently.

'Good fellow, Watson,' Holmes replied, filling the room with his enthusiasm. Then he said to Miss Copely, 'Do you know from what agency this peril will come?'

I could see that Holmes was studying this amazing woman, who had in so short a time commanded such admiration from my detective friend.

'I have no idea whatsoever, Mr. Holmes,' she said mysteriously. 'I only know that it is real. Oh, at first, I thought it some sort of perverse joke, but then the threats changed from mere words to actions. Mr. Holmes, why would someone want to kill me?'

'That is what we shall endeavour to find out, Susan,' Holmes said. I could see by his troubled manner that he realized that this was a particularly dangerous case. 'I presume that you have received letters and that you have them with you?'

'Yes,' she replied, producing a small batch of papers from her purse and handing them over to my detective friend. There were four of them and I watched as Holmes examined them intently.

'Watson, be so good as to fetch my glass.'

'Here it is, Holmes,' I said, handing him the large magnifying glass that formed such a necessary aide in his deductive work.

'This is very interesting, Susan, and you were right to come here — in fact you should have come earlier — before these threats had been transformed into actions. You are in very grave peril.'

We sat silently while Holmes continued to examine the letters. He gave a minute inspection of not only the letters themselves but the envelopes as well. When he finished, I saw the grey look of frustration etched deeply into his features.

'Well, what do you make of it, Holmes?' I said fairly bursting with curiosity.

'Unfortunately, Watson, not as much as I would like to,' he replied. 'We are dealing here with a very clever individual, one adept at covering his tracks.'

'Then it is a man who we are looking for,' I asked.

'It is a man who wrote these letters, certainly, however I believe that it is a woman behind this plot, a woman of singularly high intelligence,' Holmes said. Then he handed the letters over to me.

'Here, my good fellow, see what you can make of them.'

There were four letters and four envelopes and I looked them over as closely as I could for any signs, however small, that might lead us to some solution to this strange business.

Not much was written at all. In fact, as I read through each of the letters I soon noticed that they all held exactly the same message, word for word. The message was:

Like others before you.
You give and take away,
Now you shall pay!
Like all the others —
You shall die!

'My God, Holmes! All the letters are the same, and such a cryptic message. What does it mean?'

'I fear that we are dealing with an extremely dangerous personality, one of a sadistic and revengeful nature. You must tell me, Miss Copely, if there is anyone who has ever made a threat against your life, or may want to do you harm.'

'No one, Mr. Holmes. Really, there is no one I can think of. Naturally that was my first thought. Nor have I wronged anyone, in any manner whatsoever.'

'I thought as much, I can usually judge a person with a fair amount of accuracy,' Holmes added. I could only smile at the humility with which my friend mentioned his marvellous talent.

'Perhaps,' I ventured, 'it is another case such as that of the Ipswich Strangler?'

'A fair point, Watson,' Holmes said wrapped in thought. 'But I fear in the wrong direction. No, we must examine the content of the message more care-fully, if we do that then certain clues come to light.'

'Pray tell what they are, Mr. Holmes?' Susan Copely asked. 'This entire business is driving me mad with fear. I cannot think of who would want to torture me for no reason.'

'There is a reason, Susan. A twisted, malignant, vengeful reason it may be, but a reason nevertheless if these letters are to be believed,' Holmes said, with just a hint of doubt. 'But you are right about the torture, it is cold and calculated. The letters are worded to instil as much fear as possible. However, it is the first sentence that I am interested in. 'Like others before you . . . ' the note says. It implies there were others before you, Susan, and they are all dead now. Perhaps here we may find some kind of starting ground. For we see that this is revenge, pure but hardly simple. We are engaged, I believe, in a cloudy morass, something very ingenious, with the complications of an insane genius.'

I watched as Holmes's eyes examined our guest, his interest keen and intense. 'I take it your family does not approve of your endeavours in the theatre?'

'They never have,' Susan replied. 'They look at it as unsavoury for one of my birth and position. You know of course that my father is Sir William Copely, Lord Sedgemoor.'

'Yes, I know quite a bit about your father,' Holmes replied and I could see that it was with great determination of will that he held his emotions in check.

'He is a brilliant man . . . '

' . . . and totally unscrupulous, Mr. Holmes,' Susan Copely replied, finishing my friend's words.

Holmes made no answer to that question, instead he countered with one of his own. 'At what time did you receive these letters? In what ways were the attempts made upon your life?'

'The first of the letters came four weeks ago by the morning post. I received one additional letter for each of the two following weeks. The last one was delivered Monday last — almost a week ago.'

'And these attempts on your life?' he asked.

She sighed nervously, then regained her composure. 'There were two. I may be making too much of these letters but the attempts seemed real enough. Monday night, after I received that last warning letter, I left my home for theatre rehearsal. Up to that moment I viewed the letters as only idle threats, possibly some kind of sick prank, so that I paid no serious attention to them. I could not give into fear and let it rule me. Was I wrong, Mr. Holmes?'

Sherlock Holmes said nothing, for he was in evident deep thought.

I nodded for Lady Susan to continue her narrative.

'I was leaving for the theatre when I noticed this beer wagon race down Christopher Street. It seemed to come straight at me and would have run me down had I been in the street. I'm sure it was deliberate because I was walking on the curb and the driver seemed to come straight for me nonetheless. I would have been killed had I not been quick-witted enough to duck into a convenient doorway for safety.'

Susan continued. 'Then there is what happened to me last night when I was home making ready to retire for the evening. I walked to the window to draw the curtains and was shocked by a loud report. It was a gunshot certainly, the bullet coming through the window and missing me by bare inches.'

Holmes was still silent by this point, stretched out in his chair, smoking his pipe in intense concentration.

Finally he looked up and said, 'That you are in great danger is a fact that cannot be ignored. I do not think you have anything to fear at present, for if these attempts had been made to actually kill you, you would most certainly have been dead by now. Our London underworld is comprised of many talented and innovative individuals, unfortunately. Rather, whatever evil mind is behind this scheme is obviously trying to frighten you as much as possible. For now. It seems that your growing fear appeals to this person's own warped form of vengeance.'

'What can I do? I cannot go on living this way,' she replied and the fear that she had held in check for so long was now evident in her strained voice.

I felt great sympathy for this troubled woman, and stark rage against the sadistic fiend who was instilling fear into such a marvellous creature. Holmes too, I noticed, was not unaffected by Susan's plight, although his features were as immobile as ever.

'Have you a place to stay? Not your parent's house, it is too well known. A brother or sister, perhaps, who could take you in?'

'Yes, my brother, Albert. He has a house not far from here.'

'Fine,' Holmes replied. 'Watson will call a cab to take you there. Stay there! Under no conditions are you to leave. I will arrange matters with the official police to post a man in the house with you.'

'Will it be safe for me to go there?' She was plainly frightened now. 'If someone should be watching these rooms and follow me . . .'

'You are not in any immediate danger I can assure you, but if it will ease your mind Watson and I will be glad to ride with you in the cab.'

'Thank you, Mr. Holmes. Doctor Watson.' she added and I could see that her mind was much relieved.

2

The Ship

Once our cab left Miss Copely off at her brother's residence and we returned to our rooms at Baker Street, Holmes let out a loud sigh of dark consternation. 'This is a dangerous game, Watson. Miss Copely should have come to us sooner.'

'She is such a wonderful woman, I cannot imagine anyone with a grudge against her,' I said, watching Holmes walk over to where he kept his files and scrapbooks. There were many volumes of these old books in which he had compiled a veritable rogue's gallery of London's underworld. Finally he found that for which he had been searching and sat down in his chair opposite me.

'You are incorrect on that score, my friend, for obviously someone does have a grudge against Miss Copely. Someone we should all be taking most seriously,' he replied whilst thumbing through a book that was one of the oldest of his volumes. When he found the page he was looking for he let out a loud yell of excitement. 'Here it is, Watson! I knew it was here somewhere.'

'What are you talking about, Holmes?' I asked eagerly.

'Black Johnny!' were the only words he uttered, but I could see the loathing in his features at his very mention of the name.

'Black Johnny?' I asked curiously. 'Who the devil may that be?'

'Who indeed! The devil is an apt word in this case, Watson! Sir William Copely, Lord Sedgemoor,' Holmes replied with a slight grin of triumph.

'I am sorry if I fail to understand . . . '

'I apologize, dear Watson. I will make it all clear to you now.'

Then Holmes handed me an old and yellowed newspaper clipping. 'Read this,' he said.

SOPHY ANDERSON FEARED LOST NEAR SIERRA LEONE

[Special to The Times, Tuesday, December 16, 1867]

The *Sophy Anderson*, a barkentine engaged in the West African coastal trade was reported sunk today by heavy gales near the treacherous waters off the Crown Colony of Sierra Leone. Information is sketchy at the moment, but it is feared that all of the crew and passengers have been lost. A frantic search is now underway overseen by H.M.S. Sloop *Victorious*. As yet, of the dozen bodies recovered, only one man was found alive, though in very bad condition. The captain of the *Sophy Anderson*, master Simon MacCormic has still not been found, nor any of the passengers. Among the passengers, a vessel that carries few travellers and is used mainly in the shipment of spices, were Lord Cumberland, the new Royal Governor of Sierra Leone, who was to relieve the aged Sir Colin Wilson. Accompanying the new Governor was his wife. Lady

Augusta Cumberland and their two young sons. Other passengers were Sir Philip Harston, Mr. Alexander Kent and family, and Mr. William Copely, all members of the new Governor's staff. News of this tragic disaster . . .

'Good God, Holmes!' I replied after reading the clipping and noticing the name of William Copely. 'But this was over twenty years ago! You think this has something to do with the threats against Susan Copely?'

'It is hard to say, Watson. Knowing Sir William Copely as I do, I imagine that he is a man who has made many enemies. He has destroyed people throughout his career, any one of whom could certainly harbour a grudge.'

'I am afraid that I still do not understand, Holmes.'

'Then I shall try to explain it to you, Watson. It is a long story and one not particularly pleasant to hear.'

He relit his pipe and sat across from me, propping his long legs upon the ottoman.

'Are you perhaps familiar with the shipwreck of a vessel called the *Medusa*?' Holmes asked me quietly.

I recall hearing the name and yet I could not remember much about it. 'All I remember hearing was that some devastating horror was in some way associated with that luckless ship a long time ago.'

'Close enough, Watson, but there is much more to it and it is none too pleasant,' Holmes replied slowly.

I could see that it was a topic that gave him little pleasure.

'The facts are that in 1818 the French frigate *Medusa* went down off the coast of West Africa. Although a little before our time, there are certain parallels between the case of the *Medusa* and the *Sophy Anderson*. By coincidence, the *Medusa* also went down off the coast of Sierra Leone, but in a different area from where the *Sophy Anderson* had been lost. In the *Medusa* wreck the survivors were one hundred and fifty men who had managed to make a large and ungainly raft. It was small for so many men, so that they were forced to stand up with the wild waters of

the Atlantic Ocean reaching their waists,'
Holmes grew silent for a moment. Then
continuing he said, 'Watson, when the raft
was found by a ship and the survivors
rescued, there were pitifully few left. But
they told their tale, a tale that shocked
France and the entire civilized world, a
tale of riots, mutinies, murder, intolerable
suffering, and finally — cannibalism!'

'My God, Holmes, the painting!'

'Yes, Watson, the painting by Gericault
that we saw at the Louvre years ago,'
Holmes replied.

I could not hide the horror that crept
into my features as my mind recalled that
brilliant masterwork. It conjured images
so stark and chilling, full of struggling
emotions and fear — all the more
devastating because the events portrayed
in that painting actually took place and at
the time shocked the civilized world to it's
core.

'There were only men on the *Medusa*,
and yet their crimes and horrors will
forever terrify civilized people everywhere
— but on the *Sophy Anderson*, Watson,
there were men, women — *and* children.'

'Holmes, you are not saying . . . ' I could not bear to speak my thoughts, so full of shock and a sense of distaste was my mind in now.

'Though the case of the *Sophy Anderson* is not as well known, there are still many interesting features about the wreck that I would like to have cleared up.'

'But how, Holmes?' I replied. 'Were not all of the crew and passengers lost with the vessel?'

'As far as is known, Watson, there was only one survivor.'

'One! My God, Holmes, who was the poor man?'

'Sir William Copely is the only known survivor. Nevertheless, no sooner had he been rescued than charges were levelled against him. Charges of the most foul and shocking sort because of a diary found upon one of the bodies. Watson, the charges were so malignant that the court eventually ruled them invalid, stating that the writer, Lord Cumberland himself, had been out of his mind with starvation and fever at the time. Even the gentlemen of the press after a time, went along with 'Black Johnny' as the scandal sheets termed him then. For no Englishman could conceive of a crime so foul having been committed by any human being — much less by the son of a great English Lord.'

'And that was the end of it, Holmes?' I asked aghast. I knew my friend, and he did not mention idle gossip. If Holmes thought there was something to this story, no matter how fantastic or horrible it might be, then I was prepared to entertain the possibility that it might also be true and that there was some connection to Lady Susan's plight.

'But Holmes, what were the charges, and why was the case against Copely so quickly dropped?' I added, for now my interest was aroused as well. 'And what does this have to do with Lady Susan?'

'The charges were dropped because of a variety of reasons. Chief among them is that Copely has many friends in high places and while the case occurred more than twenty years ago, his father wielded considerable influence at the time in the higher echelons of our government,' Holmes replied, sitting in a veritable fog now, surrounded by the smoke from his pipe. 'As for how this effects Lady Susan's situation? We shall see.'

I nodded, knowing the ways of the world and how privilege too often paved the way for many in the upper class — perhaps even Lady Susan.

'The other reason was because of the problem then arising between France and Prussia which was so much in the news. It eventually brought on war months later. At that time, I seem to remember there was much debate whether Britain should aid France against the appetite of Bismarck and his Huns. In the wartime shuffle who would take notice of an event, which on the face of it, looked dubious and seemed preposterous. The crux of the matter, Watson, was that our good British public refused to believe that anything so horrible was possible by one of such exalted birth, so they ignored it and made it go away.'

'It almost makes me ashamed to be British, to see such stubbornness and ignorance. But what of the charges, Holmes?'

I could see that my companion stiffened at that, and I was shocked to see such emotion displayed in his features. I was beginning to be struck by the strangeness of this case but as yet could not see the connection that my friend obviously saw quite clearly to Lady Susan. It certainly appeared it was as my friend had told Susan Copely, that we were now entering some tangled web of horror. Then, as if to echo my thoughts, I heard the glass of the window in Holmes' room break with a resounding crash.

Instantly my companion was at the window and I saw his arms let loose with a mighty motion as he flung something into the lonely darkness of the street below.

'What is it, Holmes?' I yelled.

His mighty arms instantly wrapped around me as he pulled me to the floor of the room. 'Get down, Watson!'

Then we heard the explosion.

'Good God. Holmes! Was that a bomb?' I stammered. 'Are you all right?'

'Fine, Watson, but that was close,' he

said as he walked cautiously to the broken window and looked down below. 'Well, at least there was no one in the street at this hour. That, my dear Watson, was just too close for comfort.'

'I say, Holmes, did you see who could have thrown it?'

'Whoever it was, is long gone by now.' Holmes replied, 'but I fear that I may have underestimated our enemy.'

'What do we do now?' I asked.

'There are some hours still left until the morning. I suggest we get some sleep, for tomorrow promises to be a very busy day indeed.'

Although I was terribly shaken, I had to give into Holmes' demands and after he assured me that there would be no further attacks that night I was able to relax and assuage my anger. We were both completely worn out, and the attempt on our lives had not done our peace of mind any good.

'I need you at your best tomorrow, Watson. We must both be alert, on a keen-edged pitch.' Then Holmes wished me good night and he retired to his own room as I retired to my own.

3

Black Johnny

I returned to my room and soon was asleep but found myself in a fit of turbulent nightmare. Not the least shocking was the dream of a bomb being thrown through my own window and into my very bed as I slept. I awoke from it in a nervous sweat. I could not get back to sleep and put on a light to read until I could doze off. I left my room to get a book from the shelf in our sitting room, and in doing so passed Holmes' room. The door was open and I glanced inside curiously. I was surprised to see that his bed was empty and Holmes was not there. His bed had not been slept in, and when I looked over our rooms I could not find him at all!

Quickly I lit the lamps and walked to the closet and immediately noticed that his deerstalker and Inverness were gone.

He had obviously gone out. But where? And why at this late hour? After my initial surprise, there seemed nothing for me to do about the situation but wait — wait until Holmes returned or contacted me.

It was late morning when I heard the bell ring downstairs. Mrs. Hudson answered the door, but after a few moments I heard her voice and that of a man raised in loud argument.

'You cannot go up there!' I heard our valiant landlady shout vainly, even as I heard the tread of heavy feet upon the steps that led up to our rooms.

Holmes had said this was a dangerous business, so perhaps this man knew something of my companion's whereabouts? If so, I would endeavour to get it out of him. Before the intruder reached the top step I reached for my revolver where it was laying on the mantle of the fireplace. I quickly stuffed it into the pocket of my morning jacket just as the door to our flat was thrown open and the intruder entered.

He was a man of enormous proportions. His height was well over six feet and his build was large and muscular. He wore a great black beard that completely covered his face, but his eyes shown through like two red orbs of intense fire. His clothing was that of the well-to-do country squire, but his manner was that of an uncouth barbarian.

'What is the meaning of this?' I demanded in loud indignation. The anger and rage I felt at having our rooms broken into in this manner was evident in my speech, but it had no effect on the intruder. If anything, his face flushed red and grew more fierce. My right hand was in the pocket of my jacket holding my revolver and ready to use it should this man prove dangerous instead of merely bad mannered or loutish.

'Either get out of here,' I demanded, 'or tell me what it is you want!'

He did not answer right away, but looked around the room, perhaps looking for other occupants who might witness his dirty work, for I was sure that he had come here for no good reason. He had to be involved somehow in this business of Susan Copely, and I just hoped that Mrs.

Hudson had the good sense to run to fetch a constable should he be needed.

'Well! Speak up, man! You just don't barge into a gentleman's private rooms like a common thug. Who are you? What do you want? You know the police will be here soon . . . ' I added, hoping to shake him up — he was certainly doing the same to me.

'I should kill you!' he growled, the harshness of his voice and the rage in his face terrible to see. 'All this was none of your affair. I should kill you for sticking your nose where it does not belong. But I won't, so stop your shaking, they'll do it for me, have no worry on that account, Mr. Sherlock Holmes.'

I was quite taken aback by all this and hardly knew what to say. The man obviously had mistaken me for Holmes. My hand tightened on the trigger of my revolver and I was determined to draw the weapon and fire should he prove a threat against my person. One more step closer . . . I thought, then he spoke again . . .

'You are the cause of my troubles! If

you had kept out of it my little girl would be alive this morning,' he said, but his face and demeanour had changed now, the anger was replaced by sadness, pain. He looked on the verge of actually crying. Then he sighed deeply and sat down and I saw actual tears come to this fearsome man's eyes.

Well, I hardly knew what to make of this strange turn of events, but I realized that I had to say something.

'See here, my good man, I do not know who you are and I know nothing of your daughter . . . ' I began, still miffed at his rough manner. I feared immediately that my words were the wrong thing to say, for he suddenly stood up and I could see the anger returning to his tear-swollen eyes. What now, I thought?

'You lying dog!' he practically screamed now as he advanced, all sanity gone from his eyes now. The man was clearly deranged, but also seemed quite dangerous and I began to grow fearful even with my revolver at the ready.

'Until now, I had been content to let them do my dirty work, but now I think I shall do it myself, Mr. Holmes!'

Then he moved slowly toward me.

'I am not Sherlock Holmes!' I replied angry, withdrawing my revolver and letting him see it. 'I am Doctor Watson, a retired military man but rest assured I know how to use this weapon. Take one more step and I shall be forced to fire.'

He was not to be so easily intimidated. He came closer and I saw that all reason was gone from his eyes. Then he charged me like a mad bull so suddenly that I was unable to get off a shot before he was upon me.

I vainly tried to fight him off, but he kept coming at me, knocking the revolver out of my hand. It slid across the hardwood floor of the room and out of my reach as we struggle.

'You have the wrong man!' I shouted, trying to escape his murderous grip, trying to fend him off. 'I am not Sherlock Holmes!'

Then we suddenly heard the loud report of a firearm. Immediately my attacker let me loose and turned to face the sound of the shot. I looked up and my heart fairly leaped with joy when I saw Holmes framed in the doorway.

'I am Sherlock Holmes! You wanted to see me?' my companion asked our intruder icily. I saw he held my revolver, which he had retrieved off the floor, and now levelled it at our intruder, motioning him to sit in the chair opposite the couch.

'By God, Holmes! It is good to see you.'

'It appears that I am just in time, Watson,' he added with a grim smile.

'I would have won free in a few minutes, Holmes,' I replied lamely, but I knew the truth. I did not want to picture the results had not Holmes arrived upon the scene in time.

The intruder sat upon the chair opposite the couch quietly sobbing into his hands. He was seemingly oblivious that Holmes and I were there. The madness was gone from him now, replaced by pathetic sadness.

'But we forget ourselves. Watson,' Holmes began as his eyes examined our intruder intently. 'Where are your manners? You really should introduce me. It is not often that we have so distinguished a visitor to our humble abode as the personage of Sir William Copely, Lord Sedgemoor — 'Black Johnny'.'

I looked toward Holmes and then back at the man before us with unconcealed astonishment. So this then, was 'Black Johnny?' I could not have imagined a more bestial person.

'Black Johnny, Lord Sedgemoor?' I stammered. 'Holmes, this maniac almost killed me, and most certainly would have done so, had you not arrived in time.'

'Rest assured, Watson, that had Black Johnny wanted you dead you would ere now be spilling your life's blood away,' Holmes replied. And then to Sir William Copely he added, 'I am Sherlock Holmes. You wanted to see me? Well, here I am!'

The man, now a pathetic remnant of his former enraged self looked up at Holmes with tearful eyes, but he could not find the words to speak just then.

'It is extremely lucky for you that you did not harm my friend, Watson, here, otherwise . . . ' and Holmes left the threat unspoken. I could see that he was just as outraged by this turn of events as I, and he did not for one moment try to conceal the fact.

'Speak, man! I have little patience for roughs and scoundrels. Why have you come here?'

Our uninvited guest looked up at Holmes and myself and I could see that he hardly knew what to say, being so shaken with fear and anger. Even so, there was deep sadness in those eyes that almost made me feel sorry for him. Whatever it was, this man looked like he had just returned from a trip to the very gates of Hell itself.

Holmes handed me back my revolver and then seated himself in his chair and lit up a bowl on his pipe. He eyed the man inquisitively. 'I am waiting, Sir William.'

Sir William Copely finally got a hold on himself, held back his tears and tried to speak. It was hard for him, he was under some enormous pressure, and it was with the greatest of self-discipline that he did not break into a fit of sobs but controlled himself.

'I . . . I must apologize, to you and your friend, Mr. Holmes,' he said, and the words did not come easily to him. I could see he was a strong-willed man, one who was used to having his own way, and not used to giving apologies. 'I know that I cannot expect to be forgiven for what I have done, but I hope if I explain why I did it, then you may at least understand.'

'We are listening, Sir William,' Holmes said sternly.

'A few minutes ago you called me Black Johnny, Mr. Holmes. It is a name that I have not heard for almost twenty years.'

He withdrew a handkerchief and wiped his eyes. He was certainly in a bad way, but summoned enough energy to boldly look at Holmes.

'I take it that you will not deny meeting with my daughter, Susan, yesterday,' Sir William asked.

'It is not my turn to explain but I shall answer your question,' Holmes said. 'No. She came to me with a problem that she needed some help with.'

'Stay out of it, Mr. Holmes. If you

know what is good for you.'

'I cannot, Sir William. Your daughter is in grave danger, she needs assistance. I will furnish that assistance. There is no other way.'

'You do not understand!' Copley said nervously.

'I understand this, Sir William! Last night an attempt was made on our lives. Were you responsible?' Holmes countered harshly.

'Of course not!' our visitor said with genuine surprise.

'I think you had best come clean with this whole ugly mess, Sir William. I already know some of it, anyway, so you might as well cooperate and reveal all that you know. It would be better for you to confide in me rather than you tell the official police. I fear that they take a very dim view of cannibalism, even in our enlightened days of more liberal attitudes.'

'Cannibalism?' The word nearly flattened me, and it had a particularly horrid effect upon our guest. There was terror upon his face, horrible, gut-wrenching terror.

'So you know, Mr. Holmes?'

'I do, and you might as well tell the entire story.'

'But only for my poor daughter's sake, God rest her soul. She had nothing to do with this, nothing at all, but she has reaped the horrid results of it all.'

'Agreed.'

Black Johnny sighed deeply and after a moment of what looked to be intense concentration and tension, slowly began, 'It was the winter of 1867. I believe it was late November or early December of that year. I was one of the few passengers on the little bark *Sophy Anderson* that was bound to the British Crown Colony of Sierra Leone with Lord Cumberland, who was to become the new Governor of the area. I was a young man in those days, Mr. Holmes, and new to government service. It was more than twenty years ago that the tragedy of which I shall speak took place.'

Quickly he withdrew his handkerchief and began to wipe his brow. I could see him shaking with the strain. He was obviously a broken man, and the memories he was dredging up now were having a particularly dire effect upon him.

'There were others also on that vessel besides the crew, all members of Lord Cumberland's staff. There was Colonel Sir Philip Harston who was to be the military adjutant for the region, and Mr. Alexander Kent, who was Lord Cumberland's assistant and would be secretary of the colony.

'There were more, also, Mr. Holmes, as I am sure you know. The passenger list included Lady Cumberland and her two young sons, and the wife and four children of Mr. Kent.'

Suddenly Sir William stopped. 'Must I continue with this, Mr. Holmes. Need I paint the ugly picture for you?'

'Not for me, but for you, Sir William. Get it off your chest now,' my companion replied forcefully. 'My personal tastes do not matter at the present, I am not the official police and am not interested in a crime that occurred over twenty years in the past. Your daughter is my chief concern, and perhaps something in your story will aid me in securing her safety. She is not out of the woods yet!'

'Of course, you are right,' he replied in a voice that seemed to hold a new respect for my friend. I almost felt myself feeling sorry for this man and could hardly believe he would have performed such a loathsome act as the eating of human flesh. Then I remembered that but a short time ago this seemingly pathetic man — only concerned for his beloved daughter's welfare — had tried to murder me. Or damn near close! So at *this* point I hardly knew what to make of it all. I resigned myself to unravelling this dilemma when these thoughts were interrupted as Copely resumed his narrative.

'As I said, the ship was the bark *Sophy Anderson*, en route to Sierra Leone. The trip was slow and boring, as these cruises on small vessels often are. However, there was also trouble aboard, between Lord Cumberland and the Captain, a stern old salt named Simon MacCormic. I was not sure of the exact nature of the problem because at that time I was in my cabin and down with the fever. It had caught hold among the crew and was moving onto the passengers. I was near death for

44

almost two weeks, alone and untended, save for the kind ministrations of Mrs. Kent, who had some doctoring skills.'

'The fever you are referring to is the Yellow Fever, is it not?' Holmes queried.

'Yes, Mr. Holmes,' he replied. 'For two weeks I wasted away in that stink hole of a room. I can well remember the stench of my decaying body from the few times that I was conscious and able to understand what had befallen me. But there were other problems as well. It was not a happy ship that tread those mysterious seas Mr. Holmes. From my bed I heard gunshots one night but I'd not learn of what occurred until the following morning when Ellen, ah, Mrs. Kent, came to my room to give me some food.'

Copley stopped and sighed deeply, he was getting into the depths of it now and I could see it was tormenting him to relive those memories.

'Pray continue, Sir William,' Holmes said as we noticed the streaming perspiration upon the face of our visitor.

'It all had to do with that cursed gem, Mr. Holmes!'

4

The Emerald

'Have you ever heard of the Bagdah Emerald, Mr. Holmes?' Sir William whispered as though in fear of uttering the very name itself.

'Ah, yes. It was lost in '65, I believe. Stolen mysteriously. And I seem to recall there is a very interesting curse attributed to the stone.'

'That there is, Mr. Holmes. And you can take my word for it that the curse is as powerful today as when it was first conjured back in the dawn of prehistory.'

'Prehistory?' I blurted, not knowing what to make of all this, but bursting with curiosity.

'Yes, Watson,' Holmes added by way of explanation. 'The history of this particular stone goes far back into the biblical days. It is said that Moses gave the jewel to Rameses II, Pharaoh of Egypt, in payment for the release of the Jewish slaves from their long Egyptian bondage. When the pharaoh died many years later — for his reign was of some seventy years and he believed it was the gem that gave him the power of long life — he ordered the emerald set in the forehead of a magnificent bas relief of his image designed for the outside of his sarcophagi. It is further said that the stone is a potent talisman, protecting the owner and cursing any attacker or defiler. Rameses wanted it set there forever so that his tomb would remain sacrosanct and untouched throughout history.'

'But surely,' I stammered, 'You of all people do not believe such ... magic, Holmes?' I had never known my friend to speak so convincingly upon a supernatural subject. He simply could not believe all that superstitious mumbo-jumbo!

'Aye, Mr. Holmes,' Sir William continued. 'At least that is some of the legend, as I heard it, long ago. The stone protected Moses, though where he obtained it I shall not even try to guess. When the Pharaoh found out about it he summoned Moses to his court to show off its power. At first it is said Rameses did not believe such a talisman could exist, but soon he was forced to admit that certain of the 'tricks' the old Jew performed could not be done without supernatural aid. The Pharaoh wanted that stone and imprisoned the Jew for seven years until he would reveal its hidden location, and for seven years Moses kept silent while seven great plagues shadowed the land. Finally mighty Pharaoh was compelled to strike a bargain for the gem, that of the freedom of all the Jewish slaves and their safe exit from the land of Egypt.'

'What does this have to do with what occurred onboard the *Sophy Anderson?*' I prompted a bit too hastily, 'and with Lady Susan?'

'Be patient, Watson, we are getting there. Let us see where this particular thread leads us,' Holmes said. 'Continue, Sir William, tell us more about the emerald.'

'The stone was aboard the ship, as you have already heard. It was in the possession of Lord Cumberland. Where he obtained it, or how, I do not know, but I believe that the crew got wind of the gem and its value. It was stolen. I believe that Cumberland thought the thief none other than Captain MacCormic. You can imagine the trouble that this caused. The situation aboard the tiny vessel only became worse as the voyage progressed. I tell you, Mr. Holmes, it was the curse that caused it all, and . . . '

Holmes' face grew grim and the fire in his eyes brightened as he looked sharply at our visitor.

'I fear that this is getting us nowhere, Sir William,' Holmes grumbled. 'I told you that I want the truth!'

'Upon my honour, sir, it is . . . '

' . . . Nonsense! Rubbish! That is what it is. You are lying, Sir William, please do not insult my intelligence any longer or I shall lose all patience. Come clean with it now, you are the one who stole the gem, are you not?'

Our visitor looked shocked, as though his pride and honour had been deeply hurt.

'Come now, sir, enough of these games!' Holmes barked with impatience now.

'All right, Mr. Holmes, you are correct, I did steal the gem. It was worth a hundred thousand pounds and I could not resist it since that first night when Lord Cumberland showed it to me when we were alone in his cabin. I stole it and made it look as though the captain had done it.'

'Where is the gem now?' Holmes asked.

'Long gone, lost. I held it for years, secreted safely in my house, I thought. Then one day it was suddenly gone.'

'You implicated an innocent man?' I asked, unable to hide my utter disgust.

Sir William only nodded.

'Then you pretended to be sick, so that you could hide in your cabin, knowing full well that no one would search the room of a man with Yellow Fever,' I said triumphantly.

'Watson, my good man,' Holmes said with some surprise, 'you positively scintillate today.'

'Thank you, Holmes,' I smiled broadly

'But I fear that you may have guessed wrong,' Holmes added with a bit of a flourish.

My smile of but seconds before was now replaced by a perplexed scowl. 'But, Holmes!' I implored. 'How could I be wrong?'

'No, Watson. Black Johnny is a liar in many things but on that voyage he did contract Yellow Fever.'

'It is as Mr. Holmes says, Doctor Watson. It was the curse of that damn jewel that did it. I lay in my bed sick for weeks until finally the fever broke. Meanwhile, trouble aboard the ship was boiling to an explosive point. There was suspicion and distrust among the sailors and their captain. I had sown the seeds of suspicion all too well, and they threatened to destroy us all. I even toyed with the notion of giving back the gem. For by then I had heard the dark stories about it, the Pharaoh's curse that I believe responsible for almost killing me with the fever, and all the trouble that seemed to accompany the gem and those who possessed it through the ages. I don't mind telling you, sir, that I was in horrid fear. Finally, I did decide to give the jewel back to Lord Cumberland some days later. I would enter his cabin on some pretext, and when he was distracted pretend to find it in some secluded spot, perhaps behind the dresser. He would have his damn gem back believing it all some misunderstanding and soon all our troubles would be over. So I hoped. Little did I realize, Mr. Holmes, that in fact, our troubles were only beginning.'

Holmes was deeply interested now, no less than myself, transfixed by this man's strange story.

5

The Survivor

'I presume the mutiny began that very night?' Holmes queried. He relit his pipe and propped his feet atop his old ottoman, in a rapid and impatient gesture I had seen from him many times.

'Yes, and a horrible time it was. In the end, the mutineers were captured and killed by the captain and those who stayed loyal to him. That night one man died, and another two were hung by the yardarm the next morning, so that we found ourselves short-handed when we met the gale the next night. As things stood we never really had a chance. We found ourselves buffeted by strong winds and giant waves, which tore the gunwals out of the hull and swamped the vessel. The tiny ship foundered in the torrent and went down almost immediately. It was only by the sheerest luck that a few of us who had congregated at the stern of the ship managed to make it to a boat and get it launched in time.'

'And the others who did not make it to the boat?' Holmes asked. I feared that he knew the answer only too well.

'Dead. All dead, sir. Drowned in that horrible maelstrom.'

We were all quiet for a moment before he continued, 'Then in one of those strange quirks of fate that tie themselves with life upon the sea, the gale's great force suddenly abated. Shortly thereafter we found ourselves in a calm sea again, as we few remaining survivors struggled precariously to stay alive on that one small boat until help should arrive.'

Holmes looked thoughtful, he sat quietly puffing on his pipe. Smoke rings danced in the air around him.

'It was the curse, I tell you! My fever, the mutiny, the deaths and resulting executions, the gale and the sinking of the ship . . . all the result of the curse, Mr. Holmes. I began to feel my fate in the hands of some unknown agency, and yet all the horror I had recently been through was as nothing when compared to what would come after as we roamed those empty seas in that small and lonely boat. I am not a religious man, Mr. Holmes, but I do not lie when I tell you that I have been down into the very depths of Hell!'

I looked aghast at the man. Could it in fact be a curse? I had heard of such things from many sources, and I knew that many otherwise intelligent and educated people believed in such occult and supernatural phenomena. I looked to my friend, but Holmes sat there immobile as ever, in deep thought. What strange thoughts and Machiavellian machinations were now going on in that marvellous mind of his? Had he already solved the entire case and even now, perhaps, might he be deciding upon some manner to end this whole ugly affair?

'Well Holmes?' I blurted. I could not hold myself back any longer. 'Don't tell me you believe in all this curse business.'

At my words, Sherlock Holmes let out a small laugh. 'Ah yes, Watson, you know it has never been my way to theorize before I have all the facts. Sir William has not even begun to detail the most interesting part of his story.'

'The most horrible part, you mean, Mr. Holmes,' Black Johnny added disdainfully. 'I'd rather not talk about it.'

'But I insist that you do,' Holmes countered strongly.

'All right, Mr. Holmes,' he finally replied. 'It will be good to get this off my chest once and for all. I believe that at times confession can be good for the soul. Although in my case, I fear that events have gone too far to save any soul that I might once have possessed. I feel I am one of the damned, Mr. Holmes!'

By this time I was bursting to hear the rest of this man's strange story, yet I noticed Holmes did not press him. Instead my companion merely relit his pipe, and then folded his hands as if he were listening to an operatic soliloquy rather than the elements of one of the basest crimes in our Island's long history. Finally, he murmured softly, 'Proceed, sir.'

'Well, there were a total of fourteen of us crammed into that small boat,' Black Johnny continued, and we could see that as he dredged up these bitter memories from the burial chambers deep within his mind much pain was evidenced upon his features. 'There was no food and little water on that boat — and by the end of the third day we were all pretty well spent. At that time one of the sailors — I believe his name was McCreedy — died. The next morning Ellen Kent's two young sons were found dead in their sleep. It was horrible! There was no sign of any other ship, we were out of the main trade lanes you see, and we all knew that soon the fate of McCreedy and the two boys would overtake us as well. Ellen was badly shaken about the death of her sons and feared for her only remaining child, a young daughter by the name of Dolores. We all did the best we could but the situation began to grow ever worse and in a short time each of us felt the weakness of body and mind that presages death by starvation.

'Mr. Holmes, have you or Doctor Watson ever starved? Not mere hunger, you understand, but to be without food for many days? Do you know the feeling that takes hold of your gut, the strange thoughts that drift like mist through your mind when you are starving to death? Have you any idea what it can do to a man, Mr. Holmes!' Black Johnny said this with his usual explosive anger. His eyes blazed and I thought that I could see a hint of his old madness returning, but then he masterfully regained his composure.

'I have had some experience on the matter, Sir William. Now I must insist that you resume your narrative,' Holmes added softly, almost listlessly.

Black Johnny seemed angered by my companion's rather cavalier attitude, as I was myself. I was used to Holmes' apparent insensitivity, but really, if I did not know him better I would swear that made it seem he had no interest in these dark deeds at all. It was most vexing, for earlier he had seemed to evidence a marked interest in this case. Then again, Holmes was often an enigma to me and acted in his own strange ways for his own strange reasons. For now I had to restrain these thoughts as Black Johnny continued with his narrative.

'I fear that it was a darkness that clouded all our minds, Mr. Holmes, and that it was the gem that was responsible for the terrible deeds which were to shortly follow.' Black Johnny paused, took a deep laboured breath and then continued, 'It was a sailor named Derek Johnson who initially made the evil proposal — that we use the bodies of the two dead children for food. The thought at first revolted us all, and yet I could glimpse the hungry looks that some of my companions gave to the two small corpses. Captain MacCormic and Alexander, the husband of Ellen, also noted the silent thoughts spoken with hungry eyes by the other men. As Ellen screamed out in horror, her husband and MacCormic quickly deposited the bodies of the two boys over the side into the shark-infested waters of the Southern Atlantic. Better a hasty burial at sea in order to stave off something far worse, I am sure was their reason.

It was a sobering thought and I looked from Sir William to Holmes, seeing the disgust on my companion's face for a brief moment.

'That night the seas were calm, but not the minds of my companions. It appeared that all slept, too tired to remain awake, but their minds were scheming,' Sir William paused for a long moment, then, 'When it started, I remember hearing a mute sound, perhaps a stifled scream. In my poor condition I paid it no heed. Then later I heard a far different sound that got my attention, the sound of . . . chewing. Someone was eating! Someone had food! Carefully, so as not to awaken the others, I crept to the opposite end of the small boat. There I saw a sight that shall forever fester in the darkest corners of my mind, Mr. Holmes. There in the stern of the tiny craft was Derek Johnson, and in his hands was a large chunk of red dripping flesh!'

6

Doomed!

'Mr. Holmes, I grew crazy at the sight of food. It meant life to us all and I could think of nothing else until I saw the naked body of young Dolores Kent. Her throat had been most brutally cut and there was a large opening in her chest. Now I knew where Johnson had obtained his food. I was shocked beyond imaginings at this horror and flew into a terrible rage. Without a word I jumped upon the man. We fought briefly, for with my first blow I knocked him into unconsciousness. In disgust I lowered his body over the side — he was only good for shark bait.'

There was another pause and I thought that I could see a tear come to the man's eyes. 'Then a strange thing happened, Mr. Holmes. I cannot ascribe it to anything but my horrible starvation and hunger, and that my mind was not working in any sane manner at all. I saw the chunk of flesh Johnson had dropped in front of me at my feet. God help me, Mr. Holmes, I ripped off a piece of flesh with my teeth and began to eat it!'

Black Johnny began to cry then, as if the bursting of a dam that had held back these thoughts for so many years. Now they all burst forth.

Holmes nodded. I could see a hint of disgust upon his face certainly, but there was something else there as well, and I think it was pity.

Pity? Surely not for such a crime! Though he did not murder the girl his actions were morally repugnant in the extreme. Even if the had been starved and deranged, far better it would have been to accept death than to so debase oneself. I said as much to Holmes.

'Good, Watson,' he replied to me quietly. 'I see that your high Victorian ideals and sensibilities are not quite up to this. However, do not be too unyielding in your judgement. For you who have never known the true effects of starvation, can never understand the forces that are at play inside a man to make him do such a terrible thing. Perhaps the worst of all was not so much the devouring of the dead, but what was to come soon after — the murder of the living.'

I looked sharply at Holmes wondering what he meant by that, fearful to accept the full implications, but it seemed Black Johnny understood only too well. He looked up at Holmes trying to form his words.

I gasped at the inferance, 'What do you mean, Holmes?'

'Perhaps if Sir William has regained his composure he can continue to elaborate for us,' Holmes countered.

Black Johnny nodded slowly. 'You have guessed right, Mr. Holmes.'

'I never guess,' Holmes replied a bit stiffly. 'It is a logical extension of the facts as you have presented them to me up to this point. Please continue, at least for poor Watson's benefit.'

'Very well,' Sir William began. 'It was Captain MacCormic who was finally awakened by the sounds of the fight. He must have seen me dump Johnson over the side and watched as I began to devour the cuttings of the girl's flesh. I can well imagine the look of horror upon his face — devoted Christian that he claimed to be. Nevertheless, he came at me and there was bloody murder in his enraged eyes.

'Obviously, he mistook the entire horrible scene and thought it was I who had killed the girl and Johnson, one of his sailors. He immediately let out with a whole flurry of foul names at me that I can not even repeat to you. And as he shouted we fought like two fiends, insane and starved from hunger. MacCormic came at me like a demon, and I marvelled at the strength of the man under the circumstances. There was nothing that I could do to put him off, he would not listen to reason nor my pleas. I had no choice but to kill him. I choked him to death with my bare hands. To this day I can still feel the shaking of his giant frame as the last breath was squeezed out of him. It was a terrible thing, Mr. Holmes. Afterwards, I realized what I had done and I fear that the last thread of civilization within me snapped. Mutiny! Murder! Cannibalism! It was all too much and they would surely blame it all upon me. I had to protect myself. There was nothing else to do. There could be no witnesses.'

'My God! You are a fiend!' I shouted. 'You killed them all!'

'Easy, Watson,' Holmes replied carefully. 'We are not a court of law here. Our own feelings, however strong they may be, must not be allowed to interfere with the successful conclusion of this case.'

'But really, Holmes . . . ' I stammered. 'This was such a foul and loathsome crime. All those people murdered!' My mind reeled at the thought. I was vaguely conscious of a dizziness and a mist that seemed to cover my eyes.

I saw Holmes standing over me. He handed me a glass and I took it desperately.

'Here, Watson, drink this. It will steady your nerves.' Holmes' voice rang out reassuringly. I clutched at the glass, pouring its contents down my insides. Soon I felt the strong warmth of the liqueur giving me renewed strength. My mind cleared.

'You look a lot better now, my friend,' Holmes' voice added soothingly. 'You are possessed of rather fragile sensibilities at times. I tried to warn you of the magnitude to which this case had sunk. But there now, you look fit again. Shall we continue?'

'Thank you, Holmes, by all means continue,' I murmured.

'Please conclude your story, Sir William,' Holmes said turning to the man seated quietly upon our sofa.

'Yes, Mr. Holmes, yes, I killed them all while they slept! It was not something that I am proud of — it was a horrible thing I had to do. There is not much else to tell. I was picked up six days later. I was near death myself, but by using some of the dead for food I was able to survive.'

'I see. I suppose that you removed the evidence before you were picked up by the Royal Navy frigate?' Holmes asked with a sardonic leer.

'Yes, I had dumped all the bodies over the side. It was only later that I learned that some of the remains had washed ashore on the Spanish coast. Worse yet, somehow Captain MacCormic was not dead from our fight. He had lived long enough to be picked up by the boat of a local fisherman where he told his story as he lay upon his deathbed. There was also an entry in Lord Cumberland's diary that was later brought out at the inquiry. The gist of it was that he feared for those left alive because our starvation from lack of food and water was slowly driving everyone to a 'desperation of the most loathsome sort'. He wrote that he did not know what foul acts might perpetrate themselves on that small boat before a rescue was made.'

'And these attempts on your daughter's life?' Holmes asked. 'Do you have any idea why they should begin now, so many years after this affair? It is obvious that they are revenge against you, but since there were no survivors from the *Sophy Anderson*, do you have any idea who could be doing this? Who could know the truth?'

'No sir, Mr. Holmes. I am as much in

the dark as you are.'

Holmes smiled. I thought it odd, and I began to wonder what he saw in this case that I did not. Surely he was on the scent now. I watched as he rose and walked towards Black Johnny. 'Your daughter is safe. It was I who stole her away from her brother's house last night. I knew that her disappearance and supposed death would be the one thing to flush you out and into the open where I could learn the true story of these events. If you want to see her, then you will find her at the address on this slip of paper.'

Holmes handed Sir William the paper and then walked him to the door.

'Do not worry, Mr. Holmes, all that I care about is that my daughter is alive and safe. After I see her I shall turn myself over to Scotland Yard. Now that the story is out there is nothing for me to do, my life is at an end. At this point, I can only say thank God that it has finally come. I could not stand another day of suffering, I have lived with this for far too long.'

Holmes closed the door to our flat. I

could hear the heavy footsteps of Black Johnny as he walked down the stairs. We heard his harsh voice as he hailed a cab, and then he was gone.

7

Stymied!

A calm quiet overcame our lodgings at Baker Street as that troubled man left us. Sherlock Holmes sat silent in deep concentration, occasionally he would turn sharply to stare at a particular spot of the room, almost as if his nimble mind could see into some mysterious otherworldly realm that was forever closed to mere mortals such as myself.

Finally I'd had enough. I was fairly bursting with curiosity and fear for Lady Susan. With a bit of trepidation I walked over to Holmes and shook him back into my world.

'Holmes?'

'Easy, Watson!' he said with a hint of anger in his tone. 'I am here, I assure you. I was just concentrating on some of the more curious aspects of this case.'

'Well, it certainly has me in a blue

funk!' I replied. 'What are we to do? What are your plans, Holmes?'

He smiled but made no answer.

'Ah, I see,' I said a little disconcertingly. 'Are they so secret and complex that you cannot even tell me?'

Holmes did not answer, but I saw the smile fade from his face.

'Perhaps, it is not the proper time,' I offered nervously, seeing a strange look in my friend's eyes. 'Certainly though, when it is time, you will let me in on what you have discovered?'

Holmes turned away. He was in one of his sulking moods and I knew those only too well. I feared that soon he might begin his search for the cocaine bottle, and invariably find where I had hidden it, as he always did.

'Holmes?' I asked vainly.

Slowly he turned and inspected me with his level gaze.

'Holmes?' I asked again.

'I fear, good Watson, that this time I have failed us all.' He said it quietly, and I had trouble believing what I was hearing. Could this be the great detective that I had known and worshipped for so long? Of course it could not be!

'But, Holmes . . . ' I stammered.

'I have no plan, Watson. I fear that there is something much more hideous at work here than simple revenge, however long delayed. Whatever it is, I cannot fathom it.'

Inwardly I shook at this seemingly admission of defeat, but I tried to keep myself calm for my friend's sake. 'But, surely Holmes, you must have some theories? Conjectures?'

'None.'

'But . . . ?'

'Nothing presents itself but wild ideas, insane schemes, and . . . ' he stopped and turned his back to me and began walking to his room. When he reached the door he turned, his face seemed to have aged in that short instant, and he said, 'A bit more than murder and cannibalism took place upon the *Sophy Anderson*, Watson, quite a bit more . . . '

Then he entered his room and slammed the door securely.

I stood there alone, more alone than I

had ever been in my life, and it seemed that all the fears etched deeply into my subconscious had retched themselves before me.

What was it that had so unnerved my companion? He was a man of extraordinary intellect, a master of deduction, there was nothing that could be hidden from his marvellous mind. Or so I had thought.

Had he simply given up? Met his match? My every being rebelled at that thought, yet Holmes' action seemed to say as much. Perhaps he *had* given up? I turned the thought over in my mind. If so, why? Certainly not because of boredom, the case itself was perfect for his abilities, I realized that there could only be one answer as much as it pained me to believe it.

Fear.

But what was it that could make the greatest detective in the world fearful?

★   ★   ★

Holmes stayed in his room that day and all of the next. He did not touch the tray of food Mrs. Hudson left on the chair outside his locked door, and I began to worry more than ever.

I called to him to come out on numerous occasions and even so much as begged him to at least take a bite of food, but he would not answer my pleas nor take any food. He was being uncommunicative and stubborn as was often his wont when upon a complex case in which he could not see any immediate conclusion.

'What are we to do, Doctor Watson?' Mrs. Hudson said on the second day. 'Mr. Holmes has not touched his food, and I fear for him, Doctor. You are his friend, there must be something . . . '

'I will try,' I said lamely and reached for my greatcoat, hat and cane. Soon I was walking in the cold morning chill of the London streets.

8

Refused!

It was not long before I reached my destination. I sat alone in a magnificently attired waiting room and soon a liveried butler entered.

He bowed with practiced expert precision and said, 'Mr. Holmes will see you now. If you will follow me, Doctor.'

I walked through the warren that was the fabled Diogenes Club with awe. It was as though I were in a vast museum. Here was all that was The Empire, the greatest and most powerful men in the world were members in this most exclusive of clubs, which was as Holmes often said, much more than a mere club at all — but some type of secret extension of the Empire itself. A secret society all its own!

Soon I was brought before two huge mahogany doors. I was ushered inside and then the doors were closed behind me.

The sparseness of this chamber contrasted greatly with the extravagant furnishings of the other rooms of the club. Here there was only a long table, while at the far end sat a rather portly man whom I immediately recognized as having first met some months earlier that year.

I removed my hat, it was the least bit of respect that I could give in the presence of so important a personage. I walked forward to where he sat watching me. My mind was a mass of confusion, made more so by the fact that I noticed that this huge room did not have even one window to bring the light of day into its smoldering bleakness.

As I neared the seated figure at the other end of that long table he turned up a gas lamp that was built into the tabletop to illuminate the room. At least now there was a bit more light and I tried to gain better control over my jittering nerves for the business at hand.

The portly figure suddenly stood up as I neared him and extended his hand.

'Doctor Watson. It has been quite a while since last we met. It is good to see you again.'

I took his hand and shook it gladly, but I must admit I was a bit repelled by the strange coldness of his flesh. Mycroft Holmes was a unique man, and though he resembled my friend in many ways, there were other ways in which these two men were as far apart as night and day.

He was a large man, portly and tending towards obesity. With a balding dome upon a face that can only be described as Bacchanalian. His skin was exceedingly white, in fact it had almost a sickly pallor, and I realized that it must be as Sherlock often stated, his brother almost never left the hallowed confines of his beloved Diogenes Club.

'And how is my brother Sherlock?' Mycroft said quietly. 'Is he still engaged in his little follies?'

'Your brother is a great man who helps many people,' I said a bit testily at his condescension. Then quietly I added, 'But now I fear that he may need some help himself.'

'I see,' Mycroft said thoughtfully. 'Please tell me all about it.'

'I hardly know where to begin,' I stammered.

'At the beginning, naturally,' he said. 'Why not start with the loss of the bark, *Sophy Anderson.*'

My mouth opened and wordlessly it closed again.

'I know all about it,' Mycroft replied, and I could not tell if the slight smile that came to his lips was merely condescending or held some dark sinister implications.

'Can you help Sherlock?' I asked. 'Perhaps if you talk with him? He has hit a stone wall in his investigation and will not come out of his room.'

Mycroft Holmes smiled broadly.

'It is not a funny matter, sir, I assure you!' I stormed.

'I am afraid, Doctor, that there is nothing that I can do about this. To interfere at this stage . . . You know, I am retired now. I spend what little free time I have left to me here at the club. I do not traipse around the country.'

'Well, that is some attitude!' I replied,

my anger and pent up frustration finally finding release. 'He is your own brother, you know. The least you can do is help him.'

'You are his good friend, Doctor, and for that, and that only, I respect you. But know this, there are some things in which even the mighty Sherlock Holmes should not involve himself.'

Then he rose and made ready to leave. 'I am sorry, but this interview is at an end.'

* * *

Back through the cold and lonely streets of London I trudged, my thoughts now more confused than ever, and I knew not where to turn for an explanation of these bizarre events.

As I entered our rooms I was frustrated and angry. What kind of a brother was Mycroft to deny the help that my friend needed?

I had resolved that there was but one way to find out what was going on and the reason for Holmes' strange behaviour.

I would, as the Americans are fond of saying, endeavour to get to the answer straight from the horse's mouth. I would enter my friend's room — by sheer force if necessary — and make him confess the reason for his inexplicable inaction.

No sooner had I entered our Baker Street flat than I approached the closed door to his room. I knocked a few times, and then repeated the actions with no reply from inside. Angry now at being snubbed like this, I pounded on the door. Still Holmes did not deign to answer.

Furious now, I rammed the door with my shoulder as hard as I could. I felt the door hold rigid and firm, as I heard footsteps upon the stairs behind me.

'What's going on here, Doctor?' It was Mrs. Hudson.

'I am going to get Holmes out of there so I can talk to him properly.'

'Good. It is about time.' Then she fished her hands into her apron pocket and drew forth a key, which she handed over to me. 'I think it would be easier if you used this, Doctor. I always have duplicates made for all the doors in my house.'

'You are a life-saver, Mrs. Hudson. Thank you,' I said, putting the key into the lock. Turning it, I heard the click that indicated it was now unlocked, turned the knob, and pushed open the door. Boldly I walked inside to confront Holmes — but he was not there! The room was empty and I noticed that his bed was made and had not been slept in at all.

'My God, Doctor,' our faithful landlady cried in astonishment. 'Where is Mr. Holmes?'

'I only wish that I knew, Mrs. Hudson.'

9

Unexpected Help

There seemed to be nothing for me to do then but wait. I remained in the sitting room keeping a vigil for Holmes, hoping that he would return soon, that he was not in any trouble — but fearing the worst. I had much to think about. What was the reason for Holmes' strange behaviour? What was he scared of? Or was that but a ruse to keep me out of things? Then why? Where was he? What was he doing? Perhaps even now he was confronting our opponent? It seemed inconceivable to me that he had given up the chase and the fact that he had mysteriously disappeared seemed to support that premise now. But then where was he? And what of Mycroft's strange attitude toward his brother? Most strange. Surely he knew something he wasn't telling me. Yet, Mycroft Holmes seemed to feel it wise not to interfere. He had let slip as much. Why? That word plagued me and always the answers lay somewhere beyond my comprehension.

★ ★ ★

One more day passed since the utter disappearance of my friend Sherlock Holmes. Inquiries I made of our various contacts proved to bring about no clue to the whereabouts of my companion. Nor could the resources of our staunch comrades, the Baker Street Irregulars, yield any information.

In a state of black depression I continued to man our Baker Street lodgings hoping for some word of Holmes and yet fearing that this time that word might never come.

With Mrs. Hudson out to the vendors. I sat alone in dark thoughts when I heard the downstairs bell.

My heart fairly leaped with joy. Could it be Holmes?

Once my excitement waned, cold rationalization took a firm grip upon me once more, for I realized that it could not be Holmes at the door. He never rang the bell, and besides, he had his own latch key.

Quickly I trod the steps down to the front door. Perhaps it was a messenger with news about Holmes? If so, I would not keep him waiting, and with haste neared the door and flung it open.

It was with absolute surprise that I saw framed there in the doorway to our flat none other than Mycroft Holmes.

'Well, you may close your mouth, Doctor,' he said. 'Aren't you going to invite me in?'

'Of course,' I replied, and he soon followed me up the stairs into the rooms that I shared with his brother.

Upon entrance a slight smile came to his pallid lips as he looked imperiously about our flat with that familiar Holmesian intensity that I was so used to from my companion.

'I fear little changes in brother Sherlock's world, Doctor. These rooms are as they have always been, and knowing my brother as I do, they will probably remain so forever.'

'Well, in some areas he does tend toward conservatism,' I replied, offering Mycroft a seat which he quickly took after handing me his hat and coat.

When I returned from hanging up his garments, I sat down across from Mycoft Holmes, and I fear my features were full of surprise as I met his compelling gaze.

'Yes, Doctor, I am afraid that I am the last man on earth you expected to see tonight, am I not?'

'I must say that you are, sir,' I said, all the while feeling his eyes boring deeply into me. 'Have you heard any news of Sherlock?'

'You are a faithful friend, Sherlock could do no better than one such as you.'

'Thank you,' I said, 'but . . . but . . . '

'But I have not answered your question. Is that not so? Of course it is. However, I do not know if I can answer it. That is for yourself and Sherlock to know, I can merely furnish you with the true facts of this case.'

I nodded. Any information that might help I was ready to hear. 'So what news of Sherlock?'

'For the present he is well. How long he may continue to be so, I do not know,' my guest replied thoughtfully.

'What is it you are telling me! Is Sherlock in danger? Tell me, I beg you!' I blurted, and feared that my boldness and impetuous anger set Mycoft Holmes aback. I noticed a deep scowl set in the rigid furrows of his face at my words. But this lasted only a moment and then disappeared. I watched Sherlock's brother as his eyes roved over our rooms examining every facet of our living quarters. Finally his gaze once more fell upon me as I saw him slowly reaching into the watch pocket of his vest. With great care he withdrew a small handkerchief-wrapped bundle. He then carefully peeled open the folds of cloth to reveal a small glowing object laying boldly in the showy whiteness of the handkerchief.

Mycroft Holmes cautiously picked up the object between forefinger and thumb and held it up to the light before my eyes.

'My God!' I gasped. It was a gem of such utter magnificence that it fairly took my breath away. Beside it, such majesties as the Hope Diamond or the *Koh-i-Noor* must be content to dwell in insignificance as mere trinkets.

'It is called the Bagdah Emerald, Doctor Watson. Perhaps you have heard of it?' Mycroft said simply as he handed the gem to me for my anxious closer examination.

'It is truly magnificent!' I blurted, unable to think of words to do it proper justice. I looked deeply into it, lost now, watching the reflections of scintillating light from the myriad facets cut into the unearthly green gem. Finally I was able to reply to his unspoken question. 'I can see that it is a most unique emerald, unlike anything that I have ever seen. How did you obtain it?'

'I have my ways. It has lately come into our possession rescued from the dark rites of an Egyptian cult.' Mycroft said, with a rueful smile. Then he added, 'It is rather unique, is it not? What is really significant is that we have discovered that it has certain properties that are altogether of a very singular nature.'

'You must mean the curse? Sir William

Copely warned Sherlock and myself about it,' I added, still enraptured by the wondrous jewel. For now that I saw and held the actual gem in my hands I knew the curse surely had to be the folly of an old man too full of the guilt of his youth.

'Aye, good Doctor, what some call curse can be interpreted as something else by better minds. That is what Sherlock is endeavouring to discover this very moment. I have it on the best opinion that this gem is of unearthly origin. Come to this world in a meteor most probably. Perhaps even a new element in the periodic table? It surely must be of unearthly origin, for otherwise how can we explain its strange and wondrous properties?'

'What properties?' I asked carefully.

Mycroft smiled, 'I am afraid, that is a matter for state security at this point, Doctor.'

'I see,' I responded in evident disappointment, then added, 'Then the curse? Sherlock has always evidenced a disdain for the supernatural.'

'As well he should. There is no curse,

Doctor,' Mycroft explained a bit impatiently. 'However, there is no reason to deny that super science may not be an apt synonym for the supernatural in certain cases. All things that are unknown smell of the supernatural, yet once discovered, investigated, and rationally defined by science, become easily explainable and in fact, can become actually commonplace.

Mycroft added, 'We have such a case here with this strange gem. It is of unknown origin, yet has existed as a magical talisman of one kind or another throughout the ages. It was said by Hermith in 1451, that through the process of alchemy he could transmute lead into gold. It is, of course, an altogether improbable concept. Yet we know that for a time in 1451 Hermith was in possession of what he wrote in his journals as 'a rather luxurious emerald of curious origin which was once said to have aided the great Jew Moses in freeing his people from their Egyptian bondage''

'The emerald was in his possession?' I gasped.

'So it would seem, Doctor,' Mycroft

added. 'And if Hermith is to be believed then this gem is capable of some interesting feats. It might open up an entire new vista of science and knowledge. Once we have the knowledge to unlock the power sleeping within those mysterious facets, then there might be a newer and brighter future for all mankind.'

I was spiritually lifted by Mycroft's bold words and they did much to relieve my apprehension concerning Sherlock's disappearance. Then too, the fact that the gem did not have a curse, I must reluctantly admit, dispelled not a little of my fear. Quickly, however, my thoughts turned back to Sherlock. Where was he? What was he up to? I looked carefully at Mycroft Holmes. 'Tell me, sir, how does this all affect Sherlock? Why has he disappeared and where is he now?'

Mycroft steepled his fingers and bowed his head, much as I'd seen his brother do when in deep thought. Finally he looked up at me squarely and said, 'I fear Sherlock is dangerously involved. I fear for his safety in his secret investigations.'

'Involved in what, sir!' I demanded now. 'I must insist upon this information.'

'Of course you must, Doctor. Did I not say that brother Sherlock chooses his friends exceedingly well?'

I nodded, impatiently waiting for Mycroft Holmes' answer.

'It is a strange relationship, Doctor Watson,' Mycroft began slowly. 'Sherlock, Black Johnny, his daughter Susan, and the gem.' He looked at me carefully, 'And now the two of us as well.'

'But who or what is behind all this?' I stammered, 'And what can we do to aid Sherlock?'

Mycroft rewrapped the gem and with deft fingers handed it to me. 'When Sherlock returns, give this to him. He will know what to do with it. It is of inestimable value in this case. But have a care, it is dangerous, Doctor. Once they guess that the gem is here, they shall come for it . . . and you!'

'What do you mean? Who are 'They'?' I whispered.

''They' are the Sons of the Pharaoh, Doctor,' Mycroft replied uneasily, as though the very mention of the name was distasteful to him. Then he left his seat and went over to put on his hat and coat. As he buttoned his coat, he added, 'They are an ancient secret Egyptian cult that among other horrors perform abominable acts of assassination and ritual cannibalism.'

'My God!' I could only reply dumbfounded. What new horror had Holmes and I unearthed in this case!

'Be careful, Doctor. This is the most dangerous game of all. Brother Sherlock will explain all to you once he returns. That is . . . if he returns,' and with that dire warning, Mycroft Holmes left our Baker Street lodgings, entered a waiting cab, and was gone.

10

The Solution

Having had some service in the exotic East in my younger days — in India for instance, and Afghanistan, where I caught a Jezail bullet — I had some concept of what we were up against. It did nothing to instil a feeling of safety or confidence. My dreams were full of fearsome Sikh warriors, and of the dreadful Thuggees, murderous minions of that abominable cult of the death goddess, Kali. And now, the Sons of the Pharaoh! My blood fairly froze at the thought of what they might portend. And here was I alone, and holding the Bagdah Emerald which they seemed to covet above all things.

Filled with these worrisome thoughts, I hardly noticed the ringing of the bell that announced company at the door below. Quickly I hid the gem under the cushion of Holmes' favourite chair and rushed downstairs to answer the door, Mrs. Hudson not having yet returned from the market. In my pocket my hand was nervously upon my revolver while my free hand carefully undid the bolt and allowed the door to slowly swing open.

I looked nervously at the figure framed in the doorway and then I fairly jumped forward with excitement and relief. 'Holmes!' I cried. 'My God, Holmes! Is it truly you? Are you well?'

'Easy, Watson,' Sherlock Holmes said with a smile as he entered the foyer. He was followed by Black Johnny — and I noticed that Inspector Lestrade of Scotland Yard and two constables were also in attendance.

When we were all up in our rooms. Holmes looked to me and began, 'There is not much time so I shall move quickly, Watson. To update you, I have seen Mycroft and he has told me the little he has found out for me,' my companion said as he moved about on the cushion until his questing fingers withdrew a small handkerchief-wrapped bundle. In it was the gem I had hidden but minutes before.

Holmes looked at me and allowed an amused grin to escape his lips.

I felt embarrassed. He had found my hiding place for the gem without even trying.

We all watched in rapt fascination as Sherlock Holmes unwrapped the white cloth and pulled out the naked stone, which he immediately dropped into his jacket pocket. 'I will hold onto this for now. Meanwhile, Watson, I feel you are owed an explanation for my rather bizarre behaviour, and I shall endeavour to explain it to you in the little time remaining. For you see, we are expecting company here soon — and of a very unsavoury sort.'

'That is why I am here, Doctor,' Lestrade said. He nodded to his two men, then looked carefully at Sir William Copely. 'And to keep an eye on that one. It's good to know that after all these years Black Johnny will finally come to book.'

'Please, Holmes,' I asked quietly. 'I am afraid that I understand all too little of this event.'

'It is quite confusing, Watson, so have

no fear on that score, but I shall try my best to clear it up for you now,' Holmes said as he began to light his pipe. 'Sir William, I am sure you will add in any important omissions I may have missed?'

Black Johnny only nodded solemnly.

'Good!' Holmes said, puffing on his pipe with eagerness now. 'Well, Watson, I am sure Mycroft mentioned to you the Sons of the Pharaoh. They are a cult of criminals, assassins and worse. How much worse few in our modern society today would believe, old friend. They practice the abomination of ritual canni-balism as a way of maintaining discipline, silence, terror, and complete obedience among the membership of their secret society. It will come as a great shock to you, but our lovely Susan, Sir William's beloved daughter, is in actuality the high priestess of this nefarious sect.'

I reeled in shock from the impact of Holmes' words. It could not be! There had to be some mistake and I was about to utter my objections when Holmes held up his hand to stay my words.

'Watson, it was Susan who stole the

gem for the cult — she stole it from her own father! Then when the greed and power lust overcame her — she stole it from the Sons of the Pharaoh to keep herself — and then Mycroft's own agents stole it from her! Now agents of the cult are after the gem *and* her. Soon they will come here for both.'

'But, Holmes!' I stammered, 'she is such a lovely creature. How could she be so involved in this web of terror?' I was shocked to my very being at this news and yet how could I dispute the great detective's words? Holmes was never wrong! None knew that better than I.

'I am afraid she is deeply involved, Watson, there can be no doubt. And if I am not mistaken, she will be here soon enough,' Holmes added.

Soon after, there was a ringing from below and we heard Mrs. Hudson let the girl into the foyer. I heard her light footsteps as she walked up the stairs to our rooms.

'Susan!' Black Johnny exclaimed. 'I thought I would never see my darling again.' Then he grabbed her in his large beefy arms hugging her lovingly. I watched with much curiosity at Susan's cold and inexplicable unresponsiveness.

'You see, Watson,' Holmes explained quietly, 'he loves but one thing in life — his daughter. He can forgive her anything. Unfortunately, it appears that the feeling is not reciprocated.'

'Aye, Mr. Holmes,' Black Johnny said. 'I love her, at least enough to forgive her for stealing a priceless gem from me, which I obtained by theft in the first place.'

'And you, Susan?' I asked in disappointed anger, 'These Sons of the Pharaoh — is it really true? How could you be involved with such a group of murderers . . . degenerates . . . '

Susan Copely smiled demurely, cold and defiant. 'I am sorry that I cannot live up to your own narrow ideal of the noble Victorian woman, Doctor Watson. Truly sorry, but you see, there has never been anything that I can do about it.' Then she looked over at Holmes and Lestrade, 'Am I under arrest?'

She deftly disengaged from her father

and stood calmly aloof. 'I see that Inspector Lestrade is here. If I am not under arrest then I wish to leave here immediately.'

Lestrade shrugged, looked over at Sir William who was giving the Scotland Yard officer a stern look, 'At this time, Mr. Holmes, I fear I haven't enough to hold her.'

Susan Copely smiled victorious, turned to Holmes, 'I received your note and came as instructed, but now I see there is no reason why I should remain.'

'Indeed, Susan,' Holmes smiled and withdrew the glorious Bagdah Emerald, that until that moment, had been hidden in his pocket. 'Is this not what you prize above all things?'

We were all shocked to see what can only be described as an almost animal transformation take place in the girl before us. It was really quite amazing and instantaneous. Her eyes inflamed with lust and greed and we could barely believe that it was the same sweet woman who had come to us so recently for aid.

'I shall take that!' she exclaimed in a

dusky tone, and before anyone could move she had grasped the gem from Holmes' fingers and was out the door and down the steps before any of us realized what had happened.

'Great God, Holmes!' I shouted. 'Lestrade, we must get after her — she must not be allowed to get away with this!'

'Easy, Watson,' Holmes said motioning us all to the front window. There we saw Susan running across Baker Street, but before she reached the other side of the curb, she was set upon by four foreign-looking men. They had weapons and were clearly members of the Sons of the Pharaoh — and they were after the gem and their errant high priestess.

'Excuse me, Doctor Watson,' Lestrade said, elbowing me aside and opening the window. Instantly he withdrew a small police whistle and blew it resoundingly over and over. Immediately a dozen staunch London bobbies came out from their hiding places in doorways all along Baker Street. In no time they had all four men and Susan

Copely securely bound. I saw that Inspector Gregson was below — he had the gem and was coming up, once he had seen to the wagons loading Susan and the four assassins for shipment to Scotland Yard.

'You did a fine job, Gregson,' Holmes said, congratulating the young officer, even Lestrade acknowledged the fact with a mild nod of his head. Inspector Gregson gave the gem back to Holmes, who replied, 'Thank you, Inspector, my brother Mycroft will be wanting this little bauble back I suspect.'

Once more the doorbell rang and Mrs. Hudson announced Mycroft Holmes, his ponderous weight making the stairs creek as he climbed them in little gasps of breath.

He took out a spotless white handkerchief and wiped his sweaty forehead, then he looked at Sherlock carefully with his cold and calculating eye. 'Ah, brother, it is good to see you alive and well after all.' Then he saw the gem and smiled, 'And I see the case is solved and the gem is safe and ready to go back to the laboratories.'

Sherlock Holmes handed the mysterious emerald to his brother and with a bow Mycroft Holmes withdrew from our rooms and was soon gone.

'Well, Holmes,' I said, 'it is good to see an end to this terrible affair. I expect it is off to prison with Black Johnny . . . '

' . . . And his daughter,' Holmes pursed his lips, continuing my words. 'Such a waste. Susan had so much to offer but she never really had a chance.'

'What will happen to her, Holmes?' I asked with a far greater concern than I thought I could muster for one such as she. It was obvious to me now that her consulting Holmes in the first place had been but a ruse to get back the gem.

'She will get what she deserves, Doctor,' Lestrade answered, none too kindly. Then he and his men left taking Black Johnny with them.

'She's my daughter, my only child, and I love her,' Black Johnny said to us as Lestrade's men took him away.

'And a more vicious woman never lived! I have seen her handiwork first-hand in Limehouse,' Lestrade added pointedly. Then he paused at the door and looked over to me and said, 'Doctor Watson, she is heavily involved in numerous criminal activities — paramount of which is the diabolical sacrificial murder of a dozen victims for this horrible cult of hers. You see, she was the high priestess, Doctor. Perhaps you will understand what I am trying to say, when I tell you that it was her blade which slit the throats of the luckless victims used in the cult's ritual cannibalism.'

I turned away. There were no words to express how crushed I felt at that moment.

'Indeed!' Sherlock Holmes said, and I could feel his eyes looking upon me carefully. 'But buck up, Watson, we have brought a killer to book, and solved a crime decades old that has screamed for justice for these twenty years.'

I looked over at my friend curiously with an unasked question upon my lips, but he continued, before I could ask it.

'And yet, it was a case which had some of those stranger elements which so

103

interest me. You see, Watson, there is one thing which Black Johnny never told anyone — there was one other survivor of that hapless ship the *Sophy Anderson*.'

'Susan?' I asked, fearing his response.

'Yes, Susan,' Holmes said softly.

'But, Holmes, that was over twenty years ago — she would have been a mere child, only eight or nine years . . . '

'Exactly, Watson, but she was in that boat, and she was a party to all that happened there. Her father kept her alive, but at the cost of all the others . . . '

'How terrible it must have been for such a poor child, Holmes,' I said horrified by the dark depths to which this case had descended. 'Such a young and innocent child, to see so much of the world's brutality at that age — what a terrible cost to hold onto dear life.'

'Black Johnny readily paid that price, Watson,' Holmes said sadly, 'but there was another cost. For the sheer terror those two had gone through, the killings and all the desperate measures, could only have a negative and sickening effect upon them both. It haunted Sir William all his life with a terrible guilt that he could no longer endure, while I am sure that it drove young Susan quite mad. Sir William surely saw the signs quite plainly but like the loving father he was, he closed his eyes to it all.'

'Holmes!' I replied in shock now. 'Are you telling me that this beautiful and intelligent woman . . . '

'Yes,' Holmes said sadly. 'She is evil, Watson. Diabolically deranged. She possesses a homicidal insanity of the most vile order. Intelligent and cunning to the nth degree, she almost had me fooled. For her crimes she deserves nothing less than the gallows. I shall see to it personally that she swings from the staunchest rope at the assizes.'

And with that, Holmes lit up his pipe and soon puffed away, his face a veiled mask.

As for myself, I filled a glass with Scotch, drinking it down without a thought to the burning of my insides. Though I know I cried, I could not shed a tear.

It was over now. Perhaps some day

when I am long gone this tale will be told, though I am sure no one would believe it.

Or perhaps, it is as I suspect, no one would want to believe it.

SHERLOCK HOMES
AND THE CROSBY MURDERS

Perhaps the most horrific case my friend, Sherlock Holmes was ever engaged in, was that of the Crosby family murders. Much to his exasperation, he had been called upon for consultation only after the trail had grown cold. Nevertheless, his unique analysis of the evidence not only solved the crime, but led us to one of the most brutal and devious killers since Jack the Ripper, even as it placed his career and that of Lestrade in mortal jeopardy.

Inspector Lestrade of Scotland Yard was already at the Crosby home in Marylebone awaiting our arrival on that cold day in the winter of 1894. His constables had closed off the house to the public as the murders had attracted considerable attention from the curious. There had begun to be the most morbid and unsavoury fascination, which the popular press had churned into a positive frenzy amongst a certain element of the public.

'Good of you to come, Mr. Holmes, and Doctor,' Lestrade said as we shook hands. 'Glad you could make it on such short notice.'

'Think nothing of it, Lestrade,' Holmes said tartly. I could see it still stung my friend not to have been called in upon the case from the very beginning. However, I noticed a twinkle in his eyes now that he was finally to get down to business. 'So, what do you have for us?'

'Nasty one this time, I'm afraid,' Lestrade said, leading us into the house. 'Of course you've read about it in the papers?'

I nodded. Londoners had not been so shocked or fascinated with a crime since the Ripper killings back in '88. The horrible affair of the Crosby family had been much in the popular press lately and the vicious slayings had all of London talking. It was a most ghastly affair, a well-regarded banker and businessman had brutally murdered his entire family. That such a thing could happen among the well-bred upper class shook the very centre of our civilized Empire.

It had happened on the night of Sunday last. The vicious stabbing murder of Maria Crosby and the suffocation of her two young children, committed by her husband, Alexander Crosby. He had fled after his despicable deeds and was still at large, very much a wanted man. The bodies of the wife and children were discovered early the next morning by the maid, Josephina. So far, an extensive search by the Metropolitan Police had failed to turn up the scoundrel who may be in hiding, or perhaps as many were saying, he had already left the country for America, Canada, or even Australia.

'The papers say it was a crime of passion, Holmes, that Crosby was jealous of his wife's attentions from other men. He flew into an uncontrollable rage and killed her. She was younger than he, and quite beautiful, and they seem to imply she was a rather hot-blooded Spanish woman, as you know those people are said to be.'

Holmes smiled indulgently, 'Argentine,' he corrected.

'Well then, Argentine. So what do you make of it?' I asked.

'I make nothing of it. Absolutely nothing, Watson,' Holmes replied, much to my chagrin. I hoped he was not becoming difficult again. He certainly could tax one's nerves at times.

'So, have not you caught Crosby yet, Lestrade?' Holmes said to the Inspector with a hint of sarcasm.

Lestrade stopped for a moment, looked at my companion carefully and said.

'Well, no, not yet. In fact, we have no inkling of his whereabouts. That is why my superiors at the Yard have reluctantly allowed me to call you in, Mr. Holmes. From the outset they ordered no distractions on this one.'

Holmes remained quiet but I could not let such a statement go by without comment. 'Distractions?' I asked allowing my anger to show. 'How dare you refer to Holmes in that manner!'

Lestrade stepped back, 'Oh, no, never! Not I, Doctor, it is my superiors. This has been a prickly case from the onset, the powers that be want it closed quickly.'

I grunted, still heated over the matter.

Lestrade continued, 'The news has spread all over the country, over a week has passed now and nary a solid lead. The press and public are in an uproar and demanding action, but it is as if Crosby has disappeared off the face of the earth.'

'He almost certainly has left London,' I ventured, trying to be helpful.

Holmes looked at me then, making it quite plain by his words that while I may have blatantly stated the obvious, it was without any justification or evidence whatsoever.

I nodded, accepting the rebuke.

Holmes then noted where a couple of drops of blood had been marked by the police in the entrance hallway and more blood droplets leading up the stairs.

Lestrade explained, 'Crosby was surely covered in his wife's blood after he murdered her. You will agree once you have seen the murder rooms upstairs. He left an unmistakable blood trail to the front door when he fled. It is all quite clear. Blood drops appear in the hall here, a few more on the stairs, with more on the floor of the hallway upstairs leading to the murder room. I've had them all marked off.'

'Excellent,' Holmes said, adding, 'at least you have done that correctly.'

Lestrade sighed, led us up the stairs, 'Of course we have the police in all cities and counties looking for him. We've had broadsides printed with his photographic image and these have been posted at all railway stations and ports of departure, especially Liverpool, also the boat-train to the Continent. He'll not get away, but as yet nothing has shown up, not a peep.'

'What does that tell you, Lestrade?' Holmes asked softly.

The Inspector made no reply, though I could see that he took the comment as a veiled insult upon the lack of diligence of the Yard.

'Well, I'm sure he'll turn up.' I said hopefully. 'He's obviously in hiding. He may have an accomplice. Perhaps a mistress is putting him up? Or a family member?'

'He has no family, Doctor,' Lestrade explained. 'No close friends either, from what we can determine. And we have not heard anything about any mistress. By all accounts the man was entirely devoted to his wife and children, far too much, in fact. But no doubt we'll run him to ground soon.'

Holmes nodded. 'I think I'd like to see the room where the wife was murdered now. Then the children.'

'Of course, Mr. Holmes, follow me.' Lestrade led us into a large and well-appointed master bedroom. Of course, the body was not present having been taken to the city morgue after the discovery of the crime. The fact of that missing information was not lost upon Holmes as he minutely examined the murder site. Mrs. Crosby had been stabbed numerously. There was blood everywhere, on the bed also on the wall, and the floor.

'I've not had a thing moved here, Mr. Holmes,' Lestrade said proudly.

Holmes grunted, 'I see that only the most important element is missing.'

Lestrade looked at my companion, 'Well, we could hardly leave her here.'

'No, but you should have called me straight away.' Holmes stated, then adding, 'Did you have anyone take photographs of the body here, before it was taken out?'

Lestrade looked uneasy, 'No, I saw no need. Well, you know . . . I mean the case is quite simple really. It was just a matter of finding Crosby, that is all.'

Holmes nodded. 'Yes, that is all. At least you have stumbled onto that obvious point, Inspector.'

Lestrade looked deflated.

By the amount and spread of the blood, the killing had been brutal in the extreme. It had been a knifing with numerous thrusts and stabs and blood splashed everywhere.

'She was found on the bed, multiple stab wounds, ten I believe,' Lestrade offered a bit too casually for my taste. 'Obviously stabbed as she slept, poor woman.'

Sherlock Holmes looked at the blood upon the bed, as well as blood on the wall and floor without comment.

Lestrade produced a knife wrapped in a white handkerchief, which he handed to Holmes. The knife appeared to be covered with dried blood, obviously that of Mrs. Crosby.

'Standard kitchen knife, Mr. Holmes, it was the weapon that did the deed on the wife. It was taken from a knife rack in the kitchen on the first floor.'

Holmes examined it carefully with his magnifying glass, then gave the weapon back to Lestrade.

'I see no fingerprints at all,' Holmes stated with some surprise. 'The weapon was evidently wiped, or perhaps the killer wore gloves. Most interesting. You may remember that in the Borden Murder Case, in Fall River, Massachusetts, of a couple of years ago, it was said an axe was used. It was surmised at the time that the murder weapon had been cleaned, then hidden. It had never been recovered. Here, the murder weapon was cleaned, but it was found at the murder site. Correct, Lestrade?'

'Yes, Mr. Holmes.'

'Most interesting,' Holmes commented. 'Did you find a bloody rag that could have been used to wipe the knife?'

'No, Mr. Holmes,' the Inspector replied casually, 'and we searched the entire house and grounds most carefully.'

'Then the killer took it with him. Interesting,' Holmes noted, adding, 'You discovered no bloody gloves? No bloody clothing? No footprints in the blood?'

'No, and we found no bloody finger-prints anywhere in the house either.'

Holmes grunted, then proceeded to closely examine the blood on the bed and the various clusters of blood on the floor and wall.

Lestrade and I watched fascinated as Holmes moved about the bed and wall with his magnifying glass, looking for God alone knew what. He muttered quietly to himself as he went from one group of blood spots to another. Then he dropped down to his hands and knees and examined the blood spots on the floor with his lens with the same minute intensity, taking notes . . .

'The maid, Josephina, found the bodies the next morning,' Lestrade explained to me, but loud enough so that Holmes would hear his words. 'It was well-known the Crosby marriage was one of constant bickering and that he was an intensely jealous man. He must have flown into one of his jealous rages, taken the kitchen knife and murdered his wife. Unfortunately, he killed the two little children as well. However, he suffocated them as they slept, then he fled.'

'Ghastly crimes!' I blurted, 'The man is a beast!'

Lestrade shrugged, 'It's not all that

uncommon. I'm sad to say we see this kind of thing all the time with East Enders and in the poorer quarters, but when it happens amongst the quality folk it unnerves the public drastically. They demand the killer be brought to book immediately and the reports by the men of the press only make my superiors at the Yard press us harder for a quick close. That's why we need to catch Crosby. Then we can put an end to this. I hope Mr. Holmes can help us find him.'

Holmes deigned to reply, so I stepped into the breach, 'Well, I am sure Holmes will do whatever he can to help you and the Yard find this killer.'

Holmes continued to ignore us, as he examined the wall and the floor, finally asking. 'The body was found here?'

'No, on the bed, Mr. Holmes. I believe I told you that already.'

'The bed?' Holmes remarked, surprise evident in his voice now.

Lestrade nodded. We were waiting on Holmes patiently, as we were both familiar with his methods and eccentricities.

'And now the room where the children were killed?' Holmes asked.

Lestrade took us into another room across the hall. This was smaller but turned out to be a wonderful bedroom, gaily decorated with colourful images on the walls of smiling zoo animals and blocks denoting alphabet letters. It was a charming room, made all the more terrible by the juxtaposition of that cheeriness with the grim knowledge of the terrible evil that had been perpetrated there so recently.

It was a boon to me to view this murder site *after* the fact, as it were, so that the little bodies were no longer present. However Holmes was evidently annoyed by that occurrence.

I, on the other hand, was much relieved to be spared seeing the dead little ones. Thankfully, they had not been stabbed like their mother, but suffocated with their bed pillows, so this site was far less bloody. Yet the murder site did show trace amounts of blood making it obvious to all that Crosby had stabbed his wife first, then came in and suffocated his children while they slept. It was grim business, let me tell you and I for one looked forward to seeing the man hang at the assizes for these heartless deeds.

When Holmes was finished he said, 'It would have been far better had you called me immediately upon your discovery of these murders, Lestrade.'

'Well, at the time, of course, we knew we had everything well in hand.'

'Hah!' Holmes chortled. 'And what of the bodies?'

'Still at the morgue and unclaimed. Mr. Crosby has no family and the wife's family is in the Argentine. They've been notified by international telegram of course, but we can not hold the bodies without burial that long.'

'May I see the bodies?' Holmes asked.

Lestrade nodded, 'They are at the Metropolitan Police Morgue.'

'Then let us go there at once,' Holmes said.

'Before we leave, Mr. Holmes, I took the liberty of having the maid, Josephina, brought here. I knew you would want to question her.'

'Excellent!'

Lestrade smiled, beckoned a nearby constable, 'Have Harris bring the maid to the library downstairs.'

The constable trotted off and Lestrade led us to the first floor. I noticed that my companion seemed anxious and irritable and I inquired about it as we went down the stairs.

'Not now, Watson,' he replied without explanation.

However, Holmes' entire demeanour changed once we entered the library and Constable Harris brought the Crosby maid into the room.

We all could see she was nervous and still evidently much distressed by the recent horrific events. Holmes gently escorted her to a seat and then sat in another chair directly across from her.

'Josephina, is that correct?' Holmes began softly.

'Yes, sir,' she breathed deeply, a youngish woman, obviously Spanish, but not Argentine like her mistress. She spoke English with a light Castilian accent.

'My name is Sherlock Holmes and I

am going to ask you a few questions if you please,' Holmes said calmly and the maid nodded. 'I know you have given an earlier statement to Inspector Lestrade but I wanted to ask you again if Mr. and Mrs. Crosby had a fight before the night of the murder?'

Josephina looked at Holmes and shook her head, 'No, not that night, but they did argue much. Mr. Crosby was very jealous of my mistress. She was very beautiful, you know, and many men noticed her. He did not like this. She did not desire their attentions, but she could not help it.'

'As far as you know, did Maria Crosby ever entertain the advances of any of these . . . gentleman friends?' Holmes asked softly.

'Entertain? Oh, you mean . . . Oh, no! Never! My mistress was a good Catholic woman. A wife and mother. She would never do anything to bring dishonour upon her husband or her family. *Dios mio*, she had two little children!'

'Where were you the night of the murder and did you hear anything unusual that night?' Holmes continued.

Josephina looked up at the ceiling recalling memories of the night of the murder, 'It was a very bad night, we had a terrible storm and much rain. Much lightning and very loud thunder. The master told me I could retire early . . . '

'What time was that?' Holmes interjected.

'Just at ten o'clock. I went to my room at the other end of the house. I fell asleep almost at once.'

'And did you notice anything unusual?'

'Unusual? No, I slept all night, until I awoke the next day to find the horror, except . . . '

'Yes?' Holmes prompted.

'It was nothing. I remember waking up sometime after midnight, a loud noise, two or three actually, very sharp, loud thunder. The storm was terrible, and the thunder woke me up. Then I want back to sleep.'

'Could it have been a gun going off?' Holmes asked softly.

'I never thought of that. I naturally assumed it was thunder, but yes, I imagine it could have been a gun,' she said softly.

Lestrade shook his head in frustration, 'It was the storm, the thunder, there was no gun. The murder weapon was a knife.'

Holmes smiled, then asked, 'Is anything missing, or out of place, in the house?'

'Why, yes,' the maid replied. 'Mr. Crosby asked me to pack his small black leather valise with some travelling clothes. He was to leave for the mill in Edinburgh the next day. I was ordered to leave the valise in the hall the day before.'

'And did you?' Holmes asked.

'Yes,' the maid said softly.

'We found no such valise, Mr. Holmes.' Lestrade broke in. 'It is obvious Crosby planned the murder beforehand and took it with him when he fled. We checked with his associates in the North of course. He never showed up for any meeting.'

Holmes nodded, looked over at the maid, 'Thank you, Josephina.'

The maid smiled back at my companion then said, 'There is something else. I did not tell the police because ... I thought it was of no consequence at the time. I did not believe it could be possible but your questions have made me think otherwise. It has to do with the mill.'

'Yes? Which mill? Mr. Crosby owned several,' Holmes said.

Lestrade interjected, 'We found that Crosby and his partner own textile mills in Scotland and Ireland but they also have one nearby in the Midlands.'

'Yes, that is the one where they have the business office,' Josephina said. 'Mrs. Simpson is the secretary there and she came to the house sometimes to bring papers for Mr. Crosby to sign. She told me once the Foreman, Mr. Gomez . . . well . . . she said terrible things about him and my mistress . . . all rumours, you know?'

'I see,' Holmes said, 'and did you believe these rumours?'

'Of course not, but, he was always talking to her and . . . '

'What else, Josephina?' Holmes prompted.

'He is also Argentine, Mr. Holmes.'

Holmes nodded.

'Mr. Holmes, I hope you catch that *bastardo*, Senior Crosby, he kill my lovely Maria.'

As Josephina got up to leave Holmes said, 'I just have one more question to ask you.'

'Yes, Mr. Holmes?'

'Mr. Crosby, is he left- or right-handed?'

Josephina looked up. 'Why, he is left-handed.'

'Thank you, Josephina, you have been most helpful,' Holmes said as the maid was escorted out of the room by a constable.

Once she was gone Holmes boldly jumped out of his chair. 'Come, Lestrade, Watson, let us be off to examine the bodies to see what secrets they may still hold.'

'What secrets?' I asked, but I could see my companion was on a tear now and already out of the room.

★ ★ ★

At the Metropolitan Police Morgue, Sherlock Holmes examined the bodies of Maria Crosby and the two young children minutely.

'This place is a disgrace, Watson, a

mere warehouse to store corpses. Nothing of importance to solving a murder could ever happen here, in fact, valuable evidence is allowed to rot away with the decay,' Holmes said, mightily annoyed. 'Preservation of the body is crucial to the collection of evidence. But we seem lucky today, the cold winter weather of the last weeks has preserved the bodies nicely in spite of the neglect of the morgue and its attendants.'

Lestrade and I didn't know what to say. The morgue was the morgue, it was the way it was. What did Holmes expect?

Then we watched as Sherlock Holmes used a tape measure to get the distance from Mrs. Crosby's feet to her various wounds. He nodded knowingly, said, 'Now, here is something.'

Lestrade shrugged, while I wondered just what Holmes might have discovered. He certainly was being very tight-lipped today.

'The children were asphyxiated, so we'll learn little in the way of blood evidence from their corpses, yet I find that fact strange in and of itself,' Holmes continued. 'Such a killer would surely stab his children as he did the wife. Or else, leave them be entirely.'

'Or take them with him?' I ventured.

'Very good, Watson! You are on the ball,' Holmes said, then adding. 'It does not make sense to me that he smothered them.'

'Well, it's obvious, Mr. Holmes,' Lestrade pointed out quickly. 'He wanted to kill the children but he didn't want to make them suffer.'

'I disagree. Suffocation is a violent, slow death, but also cowardly. It seems the only consideration of suffering was shown to the killer himself . . . It might be instructive that he did not want to look upon their faces as he killed them,' Holmes said with a nod of his head.

'Smothering them, while heinous, may in this situation show some regard for the children,' I said carefully. 'Perhaps Crosby did not use the knife on them as he did his wife, simply because they were not the target of his rage as was she.'

'Perhaps, Watson,' Holmes replied carefully. 'You make a good point of it, but we shall see.'

Then Holmes took the murder weapon from Lestrade and using a variety of slow motion downward and upward strokes close to the body, recreated the murder. He repeated these strokes to coincide with all ten of the wounds on the corpse of Maria Crosby. As he did so he took more notes and measurements and compared those with his notes taken at the bedroom at the Crosby home.

Lestrade shook his head at the sight of all this. 'But Mr. Holmes, we already know how the murder was done and who the murderer is. What I need from you is help in finding the man.'

'Well, Lestrade,' Holmes replied calmly, 'you may rest assured that I am already well on the path to finding our killer!'

* * *

When I awoke the next morning I found my companion already up and about.

'Mrs. Hudson!' Sherlock Holmes bellowed, 'Mrs. Hudson!'

'Aye, Mr. Holmes,' our long-suffering landlady replied from the first floor foyer of our Baker Street lodgings.

'When the boy from Dulford's gets here, be sure to show him up immediately.'

'Aye, Mr. Holmes.'

'I say, Holmes, what have you ordered now?'

'Red paint, Watson,' he said with a wry grin. 'A standard enough item you can be sure.'

I nodded, and lit a cheroot. Well, it was about time, I thought. I for one was glad to hear Holmes had finally decided to brighten up our old rooms with a touch of new paint. But red?

I watched as he began to move furniture out from a corner of our sitting room and then brought over a pile of old posters and advertising broadsides.

'I had these sent over from the Regent Theatre. They should do fine.'

'Fine for what?' I asked, watching him place them with the print side down on the floor, then nailing others to the wall in the corner.

'It will not take long to set it all up.'

'Whatever are you doing, Holmes?' I

asked with some fear now that he might in fact be engaged upon one of his wild experimentations.

'I've had old Dulford mix the red paint very carefully, Watson . . . to the consistency of human blood.'

'Oh my, Holmes . . . '

'Fear not, my friend, I am glad you are up early today, as I can now impress you into my little demonstration. I'm sure that being a medical man, your observations on the matter will prove quite essential to the hypothesis.'

'What demonstration, Holmes? What hypothesis?' I asked, leery of God alone knew what bizarre experimentation he was now planning. 'Does this have anything to do with the Crosby case?'

'Good Watson, all will be made clear to you soon.'

That's what I was afraid of.

By this time in our relationship I was well aware of the strange doings of my friend and companion, Sherlock Holmes. I had seen him perform many bizarre and often noxious chemical experiments in our very rooms, but never before had I seen the likes of what I would watch him perform in our sitting room on that cold winter morning.

Holmes had recently concluded two of his most interesting cases, which I have noted in my records but would not chronicle in the *Strand Magazine* until 1904 — almost ten years later. These were the cases I would entitle 'The Adventure of the Abbey Grange' and 'The Adventure of the Second Stain.'

As both of these cases devolved upon certain stains and patterns of blood at the sites of murders, I was aware that Holmes had lately become fascinated with the subject. I must admit, I was at a complete loss as to just what he was trying to accomplish today and I told him so. He only smiled at me indulgently, without any answer to my question other than to go off on another tangential issue.

'I shall write a monograph detailing my findings someday, Watson,' Holmes chided as we waited for the delivery boy. 'Naturally, I shall credit your own contributions.'

'That's nice, Holmes,' I said absently. I

was fast realizing he had roped me into yet another mysterious experiment.

'I believe such information will be of inestimable aid to the police in translating blood evidence where a murder has been committed,' Holmes explained.

I sighed, knowing my friend Sherlock Holmes' experimental nature, this could become quite messy. I recalled years ago, back in 1881, when young Stamford had first introduced him to me. He had described Holmes then as a prospective roommate but warned me about his strange habits, saying, 'When it comes to beating the subjects in the dissecting-rooms with a stick . . . '

I remember how I had been shocked at the time to hear of this strange behaviour. Beating dead subjects — corpses! Why? For what reason?

'Yes, to verify how far bruises may be provided after death. I saw him at it with my own eyes.' Stamford had told me back then.

I smiled now remembering it all, but at the time I tried to tamp down my alarm, for I was desperate for rooms and of meagre circumstances. It turned out that would prove to be the least of the strange habits my companion had taken up because of his investigative work. I soon discovered that Holmes had a massive knowledge of poisons among other unsavoury subjects, but what was truly immense was his knowledge of sensational literature. He seemed to know the details of every horror perpetrated during the entire century. His intimate knowledge of shootings, stabbings, poisonings, mutilations and atrocities of all kinds could be most unsettling.

As we awaited the delivery boy from Dulford's I watched my companion complete his preparations and then begin pacing nervously as he puffed upon his pipe, the smoke swirling around him in a thick white fog. He was deep in thought now, most likely extrapolating who knew what experimental procedures.

'Toby may prove useful,' Holmes muttered, as he walked by me seemingly oblivious to my presence now.

'Eh, Holmes? Toby?' I asked, suddenly reminded of the huge good-natured bloodhound my companion used in certain cases.

'Oh, nothing. I have recently trained Toby in a new skill.' Holmes said quickly as he walked by me.

'Trained Toby? Whatever for now?'

Holmes ignored my question. 'Call me when the delivery boy gets here, will you, Watson?'

I nodded, watching as Holmes entered his room and shut the door behind him.

What now, I thought?

Presently I heard the most abominable scratchiness from a violin, what passed for music from my companion. I knew that playing the instrument often helped focus his thoughts when on a case. His improvisation, while brilliant no doubt, often sounded horrendous. Alley cats in heat gave off more melody and cannon fire, more harmony. I sighed, thankful the door to his room was shut, thus muffling most of the horrible noise from my ears.

I sat down in my favourite chair across the fireplace and thought of recent cases that seemed to have sent my companion on his latest obsessive tear. For with

Holmes, it could be described no other way. He often exhibited a single-minded nature that resulted in an intensive focus upon a fixed objective. I sighed, so be it, that was Sherlock Holmes, and if truth be told, I'd have him no other way.

I thought of the adventure, which I planned to dramatize some day as 'The Second Stain' and how it seemed to have begun Holmes' recent monomania. It had been a case of affairs, betrayal and national secrets, but the solution had been simple enough. Simple, that is, once Sherlock Holmes discovered it, then showed it to myself and the police. It all devolved upon a bloodstain on a carpet that had not leaked through to the floor as it should have done. Instead, the bloodstain was discovered by Holmes to be on the floor at the opposite side of the room under the carpet. That proved the carpet had been moved! Thereby hung the discovery by Holmes of the hiding place in the floorboards of the lost letters, which offered the solution in the case.

'The Abbey Grange' soon after, was somewhat different but I can never forget the words of the maid, Theresa Wright, when she told Holmes how she had found Lady Brackenstall and her husband. The maid's words still ring in my ears today, when she had said, *'Down I ran, to find her, poor lamb, just as she says, and him on the floor with his blood and brains over the room . . . and her very dress spotted with him.'*

It proved to be a most unsavoury and violent affair. A man had been murdered, the site of it was a horror of blood and gore. Captain Croker admitted to being the killer once Holmes put his evidence to him, still and all, the case held a most disturbing aspect. Holmes called it a mitigating circumstance. I was not so agreeable. The Captain was a murderer, that much was plainly true, but we could see he had done the deed to save the lady from her drunken, battering husband. In the end, Holmes had chosen to look the other way on it, after all, he was not the official police. He had no 'duty' here, no obligation to the law, save only his own personal duty to justice. Holmes believed justice had now finally been meted out to

Lady Brackenstall's beast of a husband. So the case was closed as far as he and I were concerned.

And now we were engaged upon the brutal Crosby murders and it seemed Holmes had prepared yet another of his strange experiments. The entire corner of our sitting room was prepared for I knew not what calamity.

'Mr. Holmes!' I heard Mrs. Hudson's voice yell up from below. 'The boy from Dulford's is here!'

I answered for my companion, 'Send him up, please, Mrs. Hudson.' Then I noticed Holmes' wretched violin playing suddenly stop. A moment later I saw his door open as if on cue as he walked quickly into our sitting room.

'I heard, Watson. Good man, now we can get started.'

The boy came up and set down two large jars of red paint. Holmes paid the boy and then sent him away.

'I say, Holmes, what is the paint for?'

'Watch, Watson, and all shall soon be made clear.'

Then my companion opened the first

bottle of red paint calmly pouring a small amount on the floor, where he began to beat at it vigorously with a hammer. Well, it naturally caused the bloody pool to spray all over a part of the wall in front of him. It was a ghastly mess.

'Really, Holmes!' I stammered, 'Have you lost your senses?'

However, what really drew my ire was to see him next take out a long kitchen knife and then dip it into a dish of the red paint so that the blade was completely covered.

'Holmes!' I stammered, shocked. 'That is not . . .'

'No, it is not the murder weapon, but one very much like it,' he said. Then standing facing the wall, he went through a series of upward and downward slashing and stabbing motions exactly as he had done with the wounds on Maria Crosby's corpse. The obvious result was that red paint once again sprayed all over that section of the wall in front of him.

I remember being thankful that at least he had the foresight to cover the area with the posters and broadsides, otherwise that corner of our sitting room would appear as if a ghastly murder had just taken place.

'Holmes!' I stammered, becoming worried now by his odd behaviour. Could it be that he had started up once again with the cocaine needle?

'Easy, Watson, I've not lost my senses. A murder case was recently brought to our attention and I am endeavouring to reconstruct certain aspects of what the good Doctor Hans Gross of Vienna calls 'the scene of the offence'.'

'You have recreated the scene of the Crosby murders!' I said, relieved that at least he'd not succumbed to that horrible drug again.

'The very same,' he said simply.

I watched Holmes as he took out his magnifying glass and then began a detailed examination of the paint droppings on the floor, going so far to get down on hands and knees and moving from drop to drop as if it were the most fascinating thing he had ever seen. At times like these he would often mumble unintelligibly to himself, and he did so now commenting about certain drippings and drops, some of which he said were different from others. He noted these quickly in a small notebook with a rapid jotting or sometimes meticulous drawings. Then he repeated the process by examining the paint drops sprayed upon the wall.

'I say, Holmes, just what do you think you are doing?'

'Investigation, Watson, before I ever theorize I first investigate. I gather evidence, and that alone will guide us to a true resolution of this grisly affair.'

'But what does it all mean?' I asked.

Holmes smiled, 'As I have always said, it is a capital mistake to theorize before you have all the evidence.'

'So you think the police missed evidence in the Crosby murders?' I asked.

'Yes, and from what I have read in the press, it presents some interesting aspects,' Holmes said quickly, still studying the red paint droplets intently.

'So what now Holmes?' I asked. 'And all this red paint, what does it mean?'

Sherlock Holmes stood up, 'a most

brutal murder was committed Sunday last, and the facts as reported by the police in the press make it seem quite the cut-and-dried matter. However, I wonder. There seems much that may be very wrong here.'

'Wrong? About what? Surely Crosby committed the vile murders and fled. Once he is found by the police he shall confess or be proven guilty and the case shall be closed,' I said confidently, adding, 'And that shall be that.'

'Yes, of course, that should close out the case quite plainly enough,' Holmes said with a smile.

I looked at Holmes, then at all the red paint he had sprayed on the wall and floor as it dripped from the backs of those old broadsides. It really did look like blood. 'I'm afraid you have recreated something right out of the Ripper killings.'

'Eh, Watson, now you have it, but not the Ripper killings, the Crosby murders.'

'But why?' I asked. 'What can it prove now? I admit I have read in the *Lancet* something of this new area of medicine. They call it medical jurisprudence or legal medicine, but it seems much more in my realm than in yours.'

'True, Watson, but are you familiar with Mr. Charles Meymott Tidy and his book of that same title a few years back?' Holmes asked me.

'I've heard tell of Tidy and believe some of his methods might be of use, but no, I've not actually read his book.'

'I have, Watson, and it offers invaluable guidance,' Holmes replied. 'Why his chapter on blood analysis alone is worthy of the price of the book all by itself.'

I nodded in acknowledgement, however the topic of legal medicine was then still very much controversial in my field. Medical doctors declined to be brought in to comment upon violent murders, resenting the unsavoury aspects often associated with these horrific crimes. Even the distinguished Dr. Joseph Bell of Edinburgh, declined to have his assistance on such cases made public. The association could cause scandal, even ruin a doctor's medical career.

'Of course, what I have done here today is but an experiment, merely a recreation of the murder.' Holmes explained. 'I'm looking at specific patterns in the blood and what they tell me about how this killing could have happened. As I remarked to you during the 'Dancing Men' case, Watson, what one man can invent, another can discover. The same concept applies in murder.'

'I'm afraid I don't follow all of this. Holmes. I see what you are doing but do not understand what it means, if anything.'

'Observe, Watson,' he said taking me over to the wall and pointing out some of the more unique features and patterns that appeared there as a result of his actions with the knife just moments before. 'Note the way the paint has dripped. Note the very definite patterns made when I thrust the knife up and down. I believe such patterns remain consistent with certain thrusts from a knife, and if that be true, there is a wealth of information to be gained here.'

'I'm afraid it all looks the same to me, Holmes. A bloody mess of red paint.'

'Of blood, Watson, but look closer.'

I did. He drew my attention to one particular spot upon the floor.

'Here we have blood that has dripped, as if from a killer holding a knife in a stable position, without movement. Note the drops are almost entirely rounded.'

'Yes. I see.'

Quickly he directed my gaze to another area on the floor, 'And here, is a location where the killer's knife was moved in his hand. Notice how these drippings have run? The blood spots here are not rounded at all, but oval, more elongated.'

I nodded.

'And here on the wall, remember Lestrade said she was killed as she slept? Yet note the similarities in pattern with that large pool of blood by the wall in the Crosby bedroom. It proves conclusively Maria Crosby was not stabbed in the bed at all, but killed standing against the wall. Then she was *placed* in the bed. Now, from my measurements at the morgue I can determine the height of the killer,' Holmes said, smiling now.

I tried to digest all this. 'So her body was moved?'

'Yes,' he said briefly.

'Whatever does that mean, Holmes?'

'Not sure, yet, old boy,' he answered with a grimace. Then continuing his explanation, 'Note the blood flung back from the knife as if withdrawn and then plunged into a body. The blood is sprayed in streaks upon the wall in very particular patterns. The drops are the same here and on the Crosby bedroom wall. They speak volumes.'

I nodded trying to follow his logic.

'Now see these blood spots, they all have protrusions, or points at one end.' Holmes continued. 'Note all these points appear at the same end of each drop. In every case. It looks very much like a tail, a tail that always indicates the direction of the blows or stabs.'

'Yes, but what does it all mean?' I asked.

Holmes smiled triumphant now, 'What it means, Watson, is that the blood at the scene of a criminal offence such as murder speaks to us in a language all its own. Having the corpse to examine was important when combined with the blood I saw at the site of the murder. It has enabled me to calculate the exact positions of Mrs. Crosby and her attacker, and tell me how tall the killer is, and if he is right- or left-handed.'

I listened amazed as Holmes carefully pieced it all together.

'There can be much more, I am sure. You remember my investigations on the varieties of tobacco ash?'

I nodded, Holmes had even written a well-received monograph upon the subject. He had also written an earlier one on the tracings of footprints with plaster of Paris.

'Well, I have always had an interest in blood evidence. As long ago as the case you wrote up as 'A Study in Scarlet', you may recall I announced I had developed my chemical test for haemoglobin.'

'Yes. I well remember your delight upon that discovery,' I answered.

'I am convinced that decoding the meaning of the blood clusters and droplets at the site of this murder will yield information which may yet enable us to catch this killer.'

'That may be true,' I admitted

reluctantly. Holmes' methods, as inscrutable as they often appeared to me, did make sense and more importantly, he did get results.

'Perhaps sooner than you think, Watson!'

'But what of Crosby? Why did he flee?'

'That is the question, dear fellow,' Holmes said. 'Now, I take off this bloody dressing gown, put on my Inverness cape and deerstalker cap and we make our way to the Crosby mill in the Midlands to talk to this Gomez fellow, thence, to visit Crosby's partner, Roderick Carleton.'

★   ★   ★

At the Crosby-Carleton Mill in the Midlands, Holmes and I, with Inspector Lestrade, met with the office secretary, Mrs. Matilda Simpson. She was one of those stern Methodist women, the type who seem to run a place entirely on their own and want you never to forget it. Holmes decided to question her first.

'It is terrible about what happened, but not unexpected,' she offered after introductions had been given by the Inspector.

'How so?' Holmes asked sharply.

'Well, not unexpected with Mr. Gomez sniffing around her all the time, if you get my meaning?'

'Her?' I asked.

'Why, Mrs. Crosby, of course. And they are both Argentines. You do know that?'

'Really?' Lestrade blurted. 'Tell us more.'

'Both the owners have offices here,' Mrs. Simpson added. 'They come in usually one day a week. I run the office and am responsible for all the paperwork. Mr. Gomez is the foreman and runs the mill. One day a week we travel into London to bring papers to Mr. Crosby and Mr. Carleton for their signatures, or to make reports. I have noticed several times that Mr. Gomez has what I consider an inappropriate interest in Mrs. Crosby.'

'Would you know what Mr. Gomez did back in Argentina?' Holmes asked her changing the subject.

'Yes, he told me he was a teacher. He's an educated man, I'll give him that, which is why he was hired on as foreman,' she said.

Holmes nodded, 'I'd like to speak with Mr. Gomez now. Where may I find him?'

'In the mill, outside and around the corner of this building,' she said.

'Thank you, Mrs. Simpson,' Holmes said, then we walked out to find Gomez.

★   ★   ★

We found Allende Gomez in the mill. Lestrade went inside and talked with him for a moment and then brought him out to speak with Holmes. He was a dark and swarthy fellow of medium age and rather short and stocky in build.

'Mr. Holmes, this police inspector told me that if I talk to you I might help find Maria's husband?'

'Maria? You mean, Mrs. Crosby, the wife of your employer?' Holmes asked smartly.

'Yes.' Gomez replied.

'I detect an uncommon familiarity with your employer's wife?' Holmes began pointedly.

Gomez flushed.

'You and Mrs. Crosby — Maria

151

— were just friends? Or something more?' Holmes said boldly.

Gomez's face heated red but he cooled down quickly and said softly, 'No, though I would have wished for something more, she was strictly Catholic. She had a husband and two children. We were friends and that is all. She was a lovely lady and did not deserve her husband, he was a jealous fiend. I hope you find him and he hangs for her murder.'

'Well, perhaps if you had paid less attention to his wife, Crosby may have exhibited less jealousy?' I said hotly. I didn't like this fellow at all.

'You think I had relations with her?' Gomez said angry now.

'No,' Inspector Lestrade said sharply, 'I believe you when you say you did not have relations with her. That is because she would *not* have relations with *you*.'

I added, 'Maybe you killed her because of it?'

The expression of shock on Gomez's face was plain for all to see, 'No! I would never harm Maria, I . . . '

'You . . . loved her.' Holmes completed

the man's words, as Lestrade and I both looked at my companion in surprise and then back at Gomez.

'Yes, I did.' Gomez admitted, pride fighting with the pain in his voice. 'But I don't understand, we know who killed her.'

Lestrade nodded.

'Just one more question, Mr. Gomez. Do you happen to be right-handed or left-handed?' Holmes asked.

'Why, I am right-handed,' Gomez said.

Holmes nodded thoughtfully as if coming to some decision, 'Watson, Lestrade, we are done here. Thank you, Mr. Gomez.'

* * *

Once outside the mill we discovered a man I can only describe as an idler walking around our carriage. I thought he might be a footpad or someone up to no good and alerted Lestrade.

'Get away from there!' Lestrade barked at the young man, who now explained that he was one of the men who worked in the mill and had something he wanted to tell us.

The man walked closer to Lestrade, and in a low voice said, 'I hear you are police looking for Mr. Crosby?'

'That's our business,' Lestrade told him. 'Do you know anything?'

'Well, I know who did it,' the man said. 'It was Gomez, not Mr. Crosby. Gomez wanted the Master's woman, but she would not have him, so he killed her!'

'Come here, you!' Lestrade shouted, but the man quickly ran off. Lestrade was about to run after him when Holmes held him back.

'Easy, Inspector, we have much work to do.'

Lestrade shook his head refusing to even consider the mill worker's words.

Holmes remained quiet as he motioned for us to get into the carriage.

As the carriage drove off, Holmes looked at the Inspector and asked, 'Oh, by the way Lestrade, would you put Crosby at over six feet in height?'

'Why, no, Mr. Holmes, Crosby by all accounts was a rather short man, maybe half a foot under six feet,' Lestrade replied.

'And what of that fellow, Gomez?' Holmes added.

'I don't know, he's certainly short, quite a bit under six feet as well,' Lestrade replied.

'Excellent, Inspector,' Holmes said confidently. Then he sat back and relaxed evidently now enjoying the ride.

I looked at Holmes, he was surely up to something but if he knew anything he was keeping it very close to his chest.

Later on, as the carriage returned to London, Holmes gathered more information from Lestrade about the case.

'The Crosby's were rather well set I hear?' Holmes asked.

Lestrade went to his notes, 'Crosby is owner of one of our smaller banks, a staunch business man, he is also in partnership in the firm of Crosby & Carleton Limited, clothing manufacturers. They have mills in Scotland, Ireland and as we've seen, in the Midlands. By all accounts it is a lucrative business.'

'And his partner, Carleton?' Holmes inquired.

'Roderick Carleton, he's been Crosby's

partner the last dozen years, a well-off toff, he's said to be a bit of a bounder and frequents the card clubs too much, but nothing wrong about him from our end. He also has a title, some minor nobility, a baronet I believe, nothing of major significance but with it comes considerable influence.'

'Still, I'd like to talk to him,' Holmes said.

'Well, we can swing by his house in Pall Mall, once we are back in London, if that's all right, Mr. Holmes.'

'That would be fine, Inspector.'

★ ★ ★

Once back in London, Lestrade had the carriage take us to the home of Roderick Carleton in Pall Mall. It was one of the newer brownstone and marble mansions of the new industrial gentry. A liveried butler led us through a long and winding hallway into the library where Carleton received all his visitors.

After quick introductions Roderick Carleton shook his head glumly, 'Of course I want to do anything I can to help you bring the murderer of Maria and the children to justice. It's just that, well, Crosby and I had been partners for years, it is inconceivable to me that he could have done anything like this. I hope you catch the fiend soon.'

'I assure you we are hot on his trail,' Lestrade said.

'Well, that certainly is good to hear, Inspector.'

Holmes had been watching Carleton as he spoke with Lestrade. The man seemed sincere, totally taken aback by the shock and severity of the crime as we all had been, and his partner's terrible place in it.

'Well, regardless, gentlemen, have a seat, and tell me how I may be of help to you,' Carleton offered. He had his servant bring in a tray of tea and scones and Lestrade and I availed ourselves of his generosity as we talked.

'Did Crosby have any family member or anyone else who could hide him from the police that you know of?' Holmes began.

'No, not that I know of, certainly not to

hide him. Crosby had no family, other than Maria and the children, of course. As for friends? Not really, he was very much a reclusive man.'

'Do you know if he kept a mistress?' I asked.

Holmes looked at me, rather carefully I noted. Had I hit a nerve? Or had I somehow interfered with my companion's own perusal of the case?

'Well, now, a gentleman should never really, you know ... discuss such matters,' Carleton spoke softly.

'So you know of a lady he was keeping?' Lestrade asked quickly.

'No, not anyone by name, but I certainly suspected he might have kept a woman,' Carleton said thoughtfully. 'I don't believe it would be proper to discuss such matters under the circumstances.'

'Quite right, Mr. Carleton,' Holmes interjected, adding, 'I assume being partners for so long that you and Mr. Crosby were good friends. Can you tell us something of your business relationship?'

Carleton looked over at Holmes and

smiled indulgently, 'Crosby and I have been partners for a dozen years now and own between us various mills and manufacturing plants. Crosby bought into my business through his bank with a half-share to capitalize and finance future expansion that has proved most lucrative. We work out of different offices in our mill in the Midlands, meeting with each other usually once a week when we are there. Mrs. Simpson runs the office, Gomez, is the foreman. They perform the actual day-to-day functions and report to Crosby and myself at our homes once a week. My partner was a jealous man, and one who could often exhibit a terrible temper. I'm aware of the problems in his marriage, and I am sorry to say that I feel this tragedy is somehow my fault . . . '

'Your fault?' Holmes asked.

'Yes, I should have seen the warning signs of his rage sooner. However, I never dreamed that he would take that rage out on Maria and the children.'

'And now that Maria and the children are dead and Crosby will soon be brought to book and hanged — I commend the dogged determination of Inspector Lestrade here and Scotland Yard . . . ' Holmes said with a pause for effect before he continued.

Lestrade nodded and smiled at the complimentary comment.

' . . . Can you tell me where the Crosby part of the ownership of your business will devolve?' Holmes asked.

Carleton looked uncomfortable, 'Well, Mr. Holmes, this is most abrupt and unseemly on your part to mention, but naturally as the sole owner, once Crosby is caught and hung, it shall all accrue to myself.'

Lestrade stood up, 'Well now, no need to get into this now, please don't concern yourself, Mr. Carleton. Mr. Holmes is just buttoning down every button so to speak, no offence given.'

Carleton smiled amiably, 'None taken, Inspector, think nothing of it. I just hope that you catch Crosby soon, before he kills again.'

'Again?' Holmes asked sharply.

'Why, yes. He has killed his wife and children, so to my way of thinking he has proved himself a dangerous man, a deadly and wanted man.'

I nodded. I could not disagree with his logic.

'Quite true,' Lestrade added. 'We'll bring him to book soon enough, he can't hide out forever, and may I say quite confidentially between us here, there is a rope with his name on it awaiting him at the assizes.'

'Well that is certainly good to hear,' Carleton said.

I nodded in total agreement.

Holmes merely smiled with a look I'd seen before. I wondered what facts and figures he was conjuring in that marvelous mind of his, I was sure it was going over the case from a hundred different points and angles.

Then as if the interview were at an end, I saw Holmes suddenly get up and step over to Roderick Carleton to offer his hand. Carleton offered his own right-hand and he clasped Holmes' hand.

'Thank you, Mr. Carleton, this interview has proved most instructive.'

Carleton blanched suddenly, then seemed to pull his hand back a bit too abruptly, I thought. However, he recovered quickly, and received Lestrade and I more warmly as we approached. Holmes watched intently.

'All I want to do is help, Inspector. The faster you arrest this brutal murderer and send him to the gallows, the better,' Carleton added.

'Oh, we'll get him, fear not,' Lestrade said, then we left.

Holmes was quiet in the carriage back to our rooms at Baker Street. Lestrade dropped us off, with the injunction, 'And do let me know if you have any suggestions on where we can track down this monster.'

Holmes remained quiet as we got out of the carriage and I could see that something was troubling him.

'Don't worry, Lestrade,' I offered. 'I'm sure Holmes will have information for you tomorrow, after he's gone over the particulars of the case.'

'Well, I hope so, Doctor,' Lestrade said. 'I want to get this Crosby into custody before he disappears for good or leaves the country altogether.'

Then his carriage was gone and

Holmes and I trudged the 13 steps up to our rooms in 221b.

★ ★ ★

Holmes remained silent most of the evening, sitting in his favorite chair, smoking his favorite pipe, swirling tobacco smoke surrounding him in a white fog. Forgotten now was his experiment of the early morning, the broadsides and their blood messages ignored now as he focused his concentration on the case at hand.

I knew my companion's moods quite well and sat myself quietly across from him in my chair reading the *Times*, but unable to think of nothing other than the terrible Crosby murders. Where was Alexander Crosby? Was Gomez involved? And what of the message from that mysterious mill employee? Surely he knew something? I was full of curiosity to find out what Holmes' opinion was on the matter.

After an hour passed I found myself unable to hold back my patience any longer, I was fairly bursting at the seams with questions. I decided to try Holmes with one question and see where it would lead.

'Well? What do you think about it?' I blurted.

Holmes looked over at me curiously as if just then noticing my presence, 'Oh, Watson, old boy, how long have you been here?'

'How long have I been here!' I said, taken aback. 'Why, over an hour! I've been sitting no more than five feet across from you all along.'

Holmes didn't say a word, and while I was aware of my companion's penchant for deep concentration, this was ridiculous, but I tamped down my aggravation and impatience as I formulated my question.

'So, what have you discovered?' I ventured.

'It's not what I have discovered, Watson, it's what I can prove. I find myself between the proverbial rock and a hard place. There is a very slim margin here for me to prove this case *and* have this killer brought to book. We are in very deep waters, indeed.'

I nodded, though I confess I understood very little of what he was talking about and told him in so many words. He did not respond immediately and I'm afraid that caused my impatience and frustration to get the better of me.

'Well, Holmes, really! Must you act so petulant?' I said rather angry, though I was almost instantly sorry that I had been short with him.

He looked over at me then with harsh annoyance, as if I'd interrupted some grand thought or design. 'Petulant? Acting as if a spoiled child? Very good, Watson, your vocabulary is improving substantially. Why not include your *new* word in one of your little stories?'

'Now you're being condescending and arrogant!' I stammered hotly.

Holmes stood up then and I could see dangerous fire in his eyes, but the flame died immediately once those eyes looked upon me. He just smiled then and put his hand on my shoulder, 'I'm sorry, John, I've been acting abominably.'

'Well, er . . . I know it must be this case . . . '

'No excuse, you have my apology,' Holmes said quickly. Then he added, 'And what's more, I will need your help to solve this crime, for we are up against one of the most dangerous and devious killers we have ever encountered.'

'You mean Crosby?' I asked carefully.

Holmes smiled, 'Not exactly.'

I believe I moaned out loud then, my exasperation getting the better of me, 'Well then, who?'

Holmes was quiet for a moment, then added cryptically, 'It may be someone else entirely. The problem is to prove he did it. Will you help me do that, John?'

I smiled, 'Of course. I can't say I fully understand all of your methods or reason, but you know I am behind you one hundred percent.'

'Stout fellow! I knew I could count on you!'

★ ★ ★

The next morning we picked up Toby from his owner. This was the bloodhound my companion used in some of his most perplexing cases.

I watched quietly as Sherlock Holmes sat across from me in our hired cab, rubbing Toby's furry mane, as he said quite matter-of-factly, 'You know I have trained him lately to do a neat little trick?'

'Oh, so you have mentioned,' was all I could say, wondering what it might be and knowing he would tell me in his own good time.

Holmes smiled, 'Watson, I don't believe the killer is Crosby at all, however before we proceed further on that tack we must first rule him out entirely.'

'But how are we going to find Crosby so we can rule him out? Lestrade and the entire Yard are out looking for him everywhere and they cannot find him with all their resources. What makes you think you can find him?'

'They are looking for a man, Watson. A man who has fled,' Holmes said carefully. 'I fear that should we ever find Mr. Crosby, we shall discover the man has been quite close by since the murders.'

Well, I was certainly surprised and

perplexed by this admission. 'How so?'

'That is precisely what we are endeavouring to find out,' Holmes said. 'I have given the driver instructions to take us back to the Crosby Mansion. When we were there before I closely examined the patterns of blood left by the murder of Maria Crosby. It was most instructive. Later at the morgue, her knife wounds were clear enough for me to do a re-enactment of the stabbings that allowed me to determine some interesting factors.'

'Go on, Holmes,' I said fascinated now. Even Toby was looking at the Great Detective with his big doleful eyes as our cab rattled toward the murder house.

'By measuring the blood patterns and the angle of wounds on the wife's corpse I've been able to determine facts that led, to what I call, a preliminary criminal description.'

'Really?' I asked curious. That certainly smacked of legal medicine, or medical jurisprudence to me.

'Not a description of our killer as clearly wrought as in a painting or a photograph, Watson,' Holmes said slowly, letting his words sink in. 'We're not ready for that yet. But we have important clues.'

'So the killer is *not* Crosby?' I insisted.

'The killer could *never* have been Crosby. The clues in our 'criminal description' tell us that quite clearly. We are looking for a man who planned this crime from the onset, he stands over six feet tall, is devious in the extreme, well-educated, and is certainly right-handed by the thrusts of the knife and the wounds on the woman's body. The blood patterns on the wall indicate this quite clearly.'

'That's amazing, Holmes!'

'Elementary, Watson, once you deduce what the evidence tells you. Crosby could not possibly have committed the murder of his wife and I believe he did not suffocate the children either. In fact, the man's name has been much, much maligned. You heard Lestrade yourself mention that Crosby was short, well under six feet. The maid, Josephina, indicated that Crosby was left-handed. No, I'm afraid Lestrade and the Yard are barking up the wrong tree in their belief that Crosby is the killer.'

'Then who is the killer, Holmes? It must be that Gomez fellow, he told us that he is right-handed!'

Holmes smiled, 'I admit, he seems ready made for the rope, he could have killed her because she spurned his advances, then also killed the children. He loved the woman and admitted it freely. But I ask again, what of Crosby? Did Gomez kill him also? That is a lot to chew on. While we are looking for a right-handed killer, and he fits that description, he does not have the height. Meanwhile, we know that he was formerly a teacher in his native Argentina, so he is an educated man. There is much to consider with him. We shall see, Watson.'

'Then what of that man who spoke to Lestrade at the mill? He seemed to know something, and he pointed Gomez out quite clearly.'

'Yes, he may know something, or merely be some disgruntled worker using the situation to get back at his foreman.

Or just a rumourmonger? We shall see soon enough,' Holmes said.

'Well, if not him then just who is the killer, Holmes?'

'That, my good Watson, is far and away a different matter,' Holmes said carefully. 'I would not dare yet theorize without sufficient evidence.'

'But if Crosby is not the killer, then where is he?'

'Where, indeed, Watson! Perhaps Toby can be of help to us in that regard.'

I was about to question Holmes further on the matter but we had now reached the Crosby home. He and Toby were already out of the cab and making their way into the house of death.

'Be a good man and pay the cabby for me, Watson,' Holmes said quickly. 'Then follow me and Toby inside. The game is clearly afoot!'

★ ★ ★

One of Lestrade's constables let us inside the Crosby home. It was Harris from the day before. 'Mr. Holmes, the Inspector told me to expect you, come on in, and you too, Doctor Watson.'

Holmes entered the mansion leading Toby by the leash. The huge bloodhound followed on ponderous feet as his nose sniffed repeatedly at everything, ever alert and ready to get to work.

'Holmes, what will Toby be looking for?' I asked.

'A bit of a search job,' he replied cryptically and said no more.

'Why, you don't fancy Crosby is hiding out in this very house, do you, Mr. Holmes?' Harris asked, startled by the very thought.

I looked at Holmes skeptically. Was that it? Did Holmes suspect that Crosby had been secreted in some hidden compartment or room in the house all along? I knew such things possible in houses built in the Middle Ages, priest holes and other secret chambers abounded. I asked my companion that very question.

Holmes just looked at me and Harris, his only comment was, 'We shall see what we shall see.'

Then he drew close to Toby and talked

to the dog calmly but with his usual asser-tiveness. He gave the huge bloodhound various commands and it immediately grew excited, pulling at the leash, ready to be set lose. Then Holmes unhooked the leash and Toby was off.

The dog walked quickly throughout the house and we all followed him.

'I have trained Toby well, he can detect the most minute amounts of blood. Now we shall see what he finds. Come quickly!'

Toby led us up the stairs straight into the master bedroom, naturally. It was the worst of the murder rooms where Maria Crosby's blood was still very much in evidence.

I didn't want to say anything about this yet, but I feared that my companion's plan and Toby's training, might be for naught. The dog had right off led us to a murder location we already knew about, not anything new at all, which I was sure was what Holmes was after.

Holmes however, never lost confidence in Toby's abilities. He patiently gave the dog further commands to track blood elsewhere in the house aside from this one location. And then Toby was off again. We all followed.

I grew exasperated when next I saw Toby run into the children's room. I recalled that there had been some trace amounts of blood found there, since Crosby had stabbed his wife first, then went there to kill the children.

Holmes patiently allowed Toby his head, then gave him further commands and set him loose yet again, telling us, 'The dog has been trained to smell out the distinctive coppery odour of human blood. Naturally he was first attracted to the major area of blood spillage in the master bedroom, then the next closest area in the children's room. Now that we have ruled these out, we shall see what else he can find.'

'I don't know about this, Mr. Holmes, seems the dog is lost at sea here,' Harris commented.

'We'll see,' I said a bit more confident, not giving up on Holmes, and Toby, quite yet.

'Thank you, Watson,' Holmes said, acknowledging my support.

Toby continued with his usual

regimen, quickly sniffing and walking from room to room. We followed him through the hallway. Then he suddenly bolted, running down the stairs to the first floor. He was obviously following the blood trail of drops down the stairs into the first floor hallway, but then he suddenly disappeared.

'See, Mr. Holmes, he lost the scent. He has ignored the blood drops in the hall and run off!' Constable Harris said. 'He'd better not do any damage here, you know I'm to be held responsible.'

Holmes ran down the stairs after Toby and I was close on his heels. When we got to the foot of the stairs we didn't see Toby anywhere, but we soon heard him.

'The library, Watson!' Holmes shouted. 'Come on!'

When we came to the large rolling doors and set them aside there was Toby barking at the center of the polished wood floor as if he'd seen a ghost.

'The dog's gone daft!' Harris said when he saw the scene.

My heart sank. Harris was correct. There was absolutely nothing at all on the floor for Toby to be barking at, but he was obviously very agitated. Toby was barking at nothing.

Holmes moved close to the dog, looked at him curiously, then looked at the floor carefully. Next his eyes roamed over the entire room intently examining it as if he had never really seen it at all before. We had been in this very room the other day, to question the maid, Josephina, but now Holmes looked at the surroundings as if he were viewing an alien landscape.

'Damnit, Watson, how could I have been so stupid!'

'What Holmes? What is it?' I asked perplexed, unable to understand any of this strange behavior.

But Sherlock Holmes ignored me, he was now on his hands and knees with a magnifying glass examining the floor-boards.

'Yes!' I heard him mutter softly, 'Very nicely done! Nevertheless, here it is, clear as day, Watson. He's a wily one, he's cleaned up well, but not well enough.'

I watched as Holmes examined the rest of the room. His eyes suddenly riveted to an area of the back bookcase.

'Hello! Watson, do you have your penknife handy?'

I did and handed it to him straight away. Then I stood by amazed with Constable Harris, as we watched Holmes dig out a slug from the wall wedged neatly between two bookcases.

'Blimey!' Harris whispered.

Holmes pulled out the slug of metal and held it between forefinger and thumb to show us while he examined it, 'From a Webley revolver, if I am not mistaken. One of the three bullets fired at Alexander Crosby that stormy night.'

'Three bullets?' I asked shocked.

'Yes, Watson, remember the maid, Josephina? She heard three loud bangs, she thought were thunder claps!'

I nodded, 'Then where are the other two?'

'Unless I am very much mistaken, still inside Crosby,' Holmes said as he took Toby away and put him on his leash. He gave the dog a treat, then whispered, 'Good dog, Toby! Good dog!'

Toby sat still now as Harris and I

watched Holmes continue to examine the library.

At that moment Inspector Lestrade came into the room, 'Sorry I'm late, police business never ends.'

'Inspector,' Holmes acknowledged.

'I knew you'd come back here, Mr. Holmes,' Lestrade said. 'Found anything?'

'Very good of you to come,' Holmes said, more upbeat now. 'I think we have some news for you.'

'Holmes found a bullet,' I blurted, then to Holmes I added, 'So you think Crosby was shot, here in this very room?'

'Crosby was murdered in this room, yes, Watson. Three shots; one missed, the other two killed him. He fell and bled to death right here on the floor.'

'But there was no blood ever found here, Mr. Holmes' Lestrade argued.

'And that is the interesting part of this case, Lestrade. Close examination shows there is definite blood residue deposited in the space between the floorboards and further, I have discovered tiny specks of blood upon the spines of certain of the books in the nearby bookcase. Here, here, and over here. I'm sure my chemical test for haemoglobin will verify these findings.'

'It was cleaned?' I asked in disbelief.

'Yes, Watson, and a good job it was, but not quite good enough. Our killer never took into consideration the marvellous olfactory senses of a bloodhound such as Toby.'

'But, Mr. Holmes, what you are saying radically changes our entire case!' Lestrade said, surprised and evidently upset. 'Nevertheless, you have no body for Crosby. No body was ever found. No gun either.'

'Inspector, I can prove Crosby was murdered here that Sunday night over a week ago sometime after midnight as surely as I am standing on the very spot now.'

Lestrade shook his head in frustration, afraid that his entire case was evaporating before his eyes.

Holmes continued, 'It must have been someone Crosby knew for him to let the man in his home at such a late hour. He was shot in this very room by that man and died here on the floor. His blood flowed onto the floorboards.

As Crosby lay bleeding to death the killer — according to plan — next went into the kitchen, took a knife from the rack and went upstairs to do the rest of his dirty work. He murdered the wife, multiple stab wounds, then suffocated the children as they slept. He left the kitchen knife behind as it held a connection to this house, and hence, to Crosby. After the murders he wrapped Crosby's corpse, cleaned the blood from the floor in the library, and then took the body away with him, probably in the carriage or wagon he had come in.'

'Really, Holmes, this is quite preposterous!' Lestrade said, trying to hold down his anger. 'We had this case all set and quite clear before you became involved!'

'Well you were wrong!' Holmes interrupted. 'It is as plain as that, Inspector. Crosby is not the killer. In fact, our killer is a much more dangerous and devious man. He has covered his tracks well. He murdered Crosby and then in a diabolical scheme, set the man up to be believed by all to be the murderer of his own family. I tell you, Crosby's reputation has been grievously wronged.'

'It makes sense, Holmes,' I said, 'but why? Why did the killer do this? And who is he?'

'Yes, Mr. Sherlock Holmes, we need a motive and a body!' Lestrade added quite petulantly.

'You may well ask the question who stands to gain by such a situation?' Holmes said simply, then added, 'But as to the body — I'm afraid it may be too late for that. Too much time has passed.'

Lestrade and I looked at each other, then the inspector just shook his head, 'Argh! That's just peachy! This is really too much, Mr. Holmes!'

Lestrade stormed out of the house, taking Constable Harris with him.

Now that Holmes and I were alone, aside from Toby who was lying down in the corner taking a much-deserved nap, I asked my companion, 'So what's our next move?'

'That is a good question. I have certain feelers out, Watson, and am awaiting news. For now, let us return Toby to his owner, then repair to Baker Street and we shall see what the Irregulars have discovered.'

'And what of Lestrade? He hardly believes any of this,' I countered, worried.

Holmes laughed lightly. 'Oh, the good inspector will come around, I'm sure. He's a sensible man, after all. His pride is hurt because the case has not gone his way — and truth be told, it was a close run thing. We are up against a most devious and brutal protagonist.'

Once back in our flat at Baker Street, Holmes took the opportunity to relax with his pipe as Mrs. Hudson and I cleared up the broadsides stained with the red paint Holmes had used to such powerful effect the morning before.

'You've made a right terrible mess, Mr. Holmes!' our landlady and housekeeper said, quite distressed by the scene.

Holmes only nodded, he was deep in thought on the Crosby case now.

As I looked at the various red drops and drippings I wondered what strange messages they told my companion. I was sure Holmes was onto something here with the formations of blood drops and all, and it seemed they might indicate certain important information. He had proven to me on various other occasions that from such trifles often came important evidence.

'Holmes?' I asked as I prepared to remove the broadsides for Mrs. Hudson, 'can you tell me what you see in the paint here — I mean what do the patterns tell you?'

Holmes looked up and smiled for it always made him happy to see interest by others in his research and methods. He came over to me like a young medical student eager to impress an older teacher, though of course, the reality of that was quite the reverse.

'The police look, Watson, but they do not see. I have learned to see what the blood can tell me. I have found it has much to say,' Holmes began. 'These patterns of blood, the droppings, drippings, spotting, smudges, all of it, tells the informed observer much about what happened during the murder and often much about the murderer himself.'

'But can this information really solve the Crosby murders?' I asked.

'As you saw, by examining the blood left behind at the murder site, even without a body present as in the Crosby case, many things can yet be determined. When we combine the information learned from the blood at the murder site with what I learned from examining the wife's corpse, I was able to determine the number of wounds, the location of the attacker and victim, and the height of the killer. Our killer was at least six feet tall. Crosby was well under that height. I was also able to determine the killer is right-handed. Crosby is left-handed. Therefore Crosby could not be the killer. Furthermore, the blood evidence allowed me to determine that Maria Crosby was standing when she was killed, then placed in the bed. Lestrade thought her killed in the bed. Not so. However, once I had determined she had been killed standing against the wall, the blood drops there gave up her story. All this data gives us those distinctive characteristics that will lead us to the killer. Oh, perhaps not in so many words, but it allows us to rule out, or rule in, suspects. Which is of vital importance.'

'So then, if I understand your words, you can put all this together and actually see some image of the killer? I understand it can not be a complete image as in a painting or photograph, but something more like a shadow, or an image in profile,' I asked.

'Yes, that is essentially correct. This empty shadow of the killer will dutifully be filled in as we discover more information. In that way my method works much like the developing fluid for a photograph — for with the more information we add, the more clear and accurate our picture of the killer develops.'

'And the Crosby case?'

'Most interesting,' Holmes said thoughtfully. He was calm but growing anxious I knew for he was waiting on Wiggins and the other Irregulars to report. 'I have been able to determine that Crosby did not murder his family as everyone seems to believe. The fact that Maria Crosby's body was moved, placed in the bed after her murder, is also significant. Scotland Yard has been sent on a very nicely-wrought wild goose chase by the true killer who is a master of misdirection. They have been searching for the wrong man, a man who I am sure now, no longer exists.'

'Then who is the right man?' I asked. 'Who is the killer?'

Holmes nodded, 'Perhaps we should await the news Wiggins and the Irregulars bring us before we move on further, Watson. I do have a theory but I need just a bit more evidence to close the book. We have the means and opportunity but a motive is still required, since we do not have Crosby's body.'

It wasn't long after when Mrs. Hudson let up Wiggins and three of his rascal companions into our rooms. At the same time we had a visit from a much sombre Inspector Lestrade who followed the boys up the stairs into our living quarters rather demurely.

Lestrade came over to Holmes, 'I

thought a lot about what you said. We've had everyone looking for Crosby all across the country for over a week. We've had leads, a few sightings, but all have proved false. The case is in the press overmuch I fear and people think they see him everywhere lately. Meanwhile, he seems to have disappeared far too well. I have to admit you may have something in your theory, Mr. Holmes, and your evidence does seem incontrovertible. But if it is not Crosby, then who is the killer and why such a brutal crime?'

'I can answer the second part of your question right away, Inspector,' Holmes said as he gave Wiggins a hesitant gesture ordering the boy to wait with his news.

Holmes then continued, 'The brutality of the crime is a mask our murderer set up to deflect suspicion from himself and onto Crosby. Our killer is a master at misdirection and there are numerous points of misdirection he has used in this case. By cleaning up the site of Crosby's murder in the library and taking away his body, it caused Crosby to become the immediate and only suspect. A husband is always a natural suspect in such wifely murders regardless, but our killer also knew about their marriage problems, playing upon that so Crosby became the foil for the killings — thus protecting the true killer. The fact that Crosby could not be found only made the police search all the more for him. But your search was ordained to be in vain. Misdirection, Inspector, admirably done.'

Lestrade nodded, 'That might be, Mr. Holmes, but if so, who is the killer and why did he do it?'

'Wiggins?' Holmes asked the boy who was twitching with excitement. 'You have something to report?'

'Aye, Mr. 'Olmes, I sure as 'ell do!' the young street Arab blurted with his usual enthusiasm. 'Me and the lads 'ere did as you said. We brought your notes to the gentlemen and waited for their answers.'

Wiggins handed Holmes four slips of paper.

'Earlier this morning,' Holmes explained, 'I sent Wiggins here with three of his confederates to deliver by hand certain messages to four of London's major figures who, shall we say, dabble in the quality gambling and loan enterprise.'

'Bookies and loan sharks?' Lestrade asked bluntly.

'Quite right, inspector, but these four men are not your usual street toughs or cosh boys, they are financiers of gambling for moneyed gentlemen of the upper classes. And each one of them owes me a favour. The question I put to them was the amount of debt incurred by one Roderick Carleton of Crosby & Carleton Limited. Their responses are illuminating to say the least.'

All eyes were on Holmes now, even the Irregulars who knew the results, watched the Great Detective in rapt fascination. Then he began, 'We have Patterson who reports a debt of 10,000 pounds owed; Smythe-Jones says 20,000 pounds; Filson mentions a figure of 50,000 pounds and McGregor of the old Moriarty gang reluctantly tells me that Carleton is in debt to him in excess of 75,000 pounds!'

'Blimey!' Lestrade hissed.

'Blimey, indeed, Inspector,' Holmes

repeated, then he gave each of the Irregulars a silver Sovereign, saying, 'You have done well tonight, lads.'

Then he sent them away.

Inspector Lestrade now looked at Holmes in a new light, 'Well this changes everything.'

'Roderick Carleton?' I asked, disbelieving, 'But surely, Holmes, you can't mean he actually planned this all from the beginning?'

'Absolutely, Watson,' Holmes answered. 'He was deeply in debt to some very bad people. Gambling debts, of the worst kind. He was threatened with bankruptcy and worse, serious scandal if he did not pay up soon. Perhaps even threats of violence on his own person. Then he saw his opportunity. He knew if he killed his partner the business would come into his possession. But so would suspicion unless he hit upon some scheme to deflect the murder. He was aware of the problems in the Crosby marriage, aware of the layout of the man's house, and so he visited Crosby on that dark and rainy night, the thunder booming, no one else about so late, and he did his vile deed.'

'But what of this Gomez fellow?' Lestrade asked.

'I admit he seems ready-made for the rope by some accounts, but he does not fit the criminal description I have come up with. For instance he is well *under* six feet.' Holmes said. 'And I believe he loved Maria, and could not kill her, especially in such a brutal manner . . . '

'Holmes, this is fantastic!' I blurted.

'There is nothing fantastic about it, Watson, just observation and evidence,' Holmes replied, lighting his pipe.

'Aye, Mr. Holmes, quite the fanciful tale, but Carleton is a respected business-man and a man of some influence, irrespective of his gambling debts. I would almost accept your theory, but for one thing, we have no body. Where is Crosby?'

'Where, indeed, Lestrade?' Holmes said softly.

★　★　★

The next morning Lestrade and I accompanied Holmes to Carleton Manor in Pall Mall to confront Roderick Carleton with what we knew about the killings with the inducement that the police would offer a waiver on the death penalty upon his confession.

'Our evidence is circumstantial, but it all points directly at Carleton,' Holmes said, in the carriage on the way there. 'However, I realize that without Crosby's body we are on ground here that may be as treacherous as the Grimpen Mire.'

Once at the Carleton mansion, the butler let us into the expansive house via the long hallway that brought us directly to his master, who was waiting in the library. Roderick Carleton had an annoyed look on his face, clearly not happy to see us again.

'Have you caught Crosby yet?' he asked after we entered the room, then he bid us sit down. There was no tea or scones offered us this time.

'Not yet,' Lestrade said softly. 'But we are ardently searching.'

'Well, then, what can I do for you, Inspector?'

'Mr. Holmes here, has some news for you on the murders that you might be interested in,' Lestrade said with a smile.

'Is that so? I can't possibly see what any of this has to do with me, other than the fact that I hope you catch Crosby, of course,' Carleton said softly, confidence oozed out of him.

'Of course,' Holmes mimicked, 'but did you know that we have discovered that Crosby did not actually murder his family?'

Carleton looked at the Great Detective with shock upon his face, then over to Lestrade, 'Is that true, Inspector?'

'I'm afraid so, Mr. Carleton,' Lestrade said simply.

'That's amazing,' Carleton said, quickly regaining his composure. 'I mean, from what you told me yesterday and from what I've read in the papers, I was led to believe that it was Crosby who committed these murders.'

'We have another suspect,' Lestrade stated.

'Really?' Carleton asked softly, calculating, careful now. He smiled, added, 'Someone on the servant staff perhaps? Or one of Maria's so-called admirers? There is that Foreman, Gomez, who you should absolutely talk to.'

'We've already talked to him,' Lestrade said.

'Well, then, why are you here and not out arresting him?' Carleton said defiantly.

There was a pause, a moment of intense silence, then Sherlock Holmes said simply, 'Actually, our leading suspect, Mr. Carleton . . . is yourself.'

'Me? That's preposterous!' Carleton turned red in the face and suddenly stood up out of his seat. 'I don't have to sit here in my own home and listen to these wild accusations, promulgated I may point out, by a rank amateur. Really, Inspector, I shall complain loudly to your superiors at the Yard about this!'

Lestrade seemed to grow visibly nervous at this threat. It was obvious he, and perhaps even Holmes, had not anticipated such a powerful denial and the implication of political repercussions that Carleton could bring into play. Yet Holmes remained undaunted by the threat.

'Sit down, Mr. Carleton, I am not finished yet,' Holmes ordered as he rose and walked toward the man looking at him eye to eye.

Carleton got a hold of himself and sat down again.

'You can come clean with it all now,' Holmes offered. 'If you do so now, I assure you that the death penalty will be waived in these murders.'

Carleton pursed his lips as if ready to shout but perhaps thought better of it and just sat back. He smiled confidently. 'You have nothing, Mr. Sherlock Holmes!'

'We have your gambling debts. You owe to the tune of over 150,000 pounds to some very unsavoury characters. You are in deep financial straights, which speaks of a motive. Your murder of the Crosby family and placing the blame on your partner would serve all your financial needs. It's no secret now that Crosby was contemplating dissolving the partnership because of your gambling activities. Your scheme would allow you full control of the business and what you crave above all else, the wealth of that business.'

Instead of getting angry, Carleton merely smiled, 'Even if what you say about my debts is true, that is none of your business, and it hardly indicates I murdered anyone. Many in the quality class enjoy a good wager, it is not a crime.' Then he looked at Lestrade again, 'Please, Inspector, I do not appreciate being insulted by this man's mad ramblings!'

I bristled at this insult to my friend, and was about to voice my anger when Carleton looked at me and said harshly, 'Doctor, call off your friend before I place my solicitor upon him with a slander charge. I assure you it will destroy him and his career.'

'Your threats have no effect upon me,' Holmes continued forcefully. 'I have discovered evidence that links this crime to you as clearly as if you had left your confession at the site of your vicious deeds.'

Carleton's confidence wavered just a bit, 'What evidence?'

'The blood at the site of the murder and the wounds on the body on Mrs. Crosby indicate clearly that the murderer stood well over six feet tall and was right-handed. For you see, Mr. Crosby stood well *under* six feet and was *left*-handed!'

Carleton did not say one word but we could see he was thinking it through most carefully.

Holmes said, 'You did a neat job of cleaning the blood off the library floor and of removing Crosby's body — after you shot and killed him. Mind telling us now where you hid his body?'

Carleton smiled slightly but made no comment.

Holmes continued, 'I found one of your slugs in the wood of the library bookcase, we can get a warrant to find that gun.'

'No such gun exists, Mr. Holmes.' Carleton said confidently.

'We can prove that Crosby was shot, the maid heard the reports of the weapon.' Holmes added, 'By the way, that was a nice touch using a knife from the household kitchen and then leaving it behind for the police to find. You made it all quite convenient.'

Carleton sat stone silent.

'In any case,' Holmes stated evenly, 'Crosby was shot and killed by you in the library. Your cleaning of the blood was good, but not good enough. I discovered residue blood between the floorboards and tiny spots of blood upon the spines of some of the books in the bookcase. Crosby was murdered in that room, it was cleaned afterwards and you took away the body. Your plan was to make Crosby take the fall as the natural suspect. The fact that he had apparently fled after the murders, with a bag already packed, only caused the police to accept your plan all the more.'

'This is ridiculous!' Carleton stammered in rage, but I thought I could see worry growing on his face now also.

'You set this up from the very beginning to take control of the business,' Holmes continued. 'You had inside knowledge of the Crosby marriage and your partner's temper which you used to your advantage. You knew the layout of the house. You came there late that Sunday night, probably upon some pretext to do with one of the mills. You knew Crosby would admit you, and he did.'

'Inspector?' Carleton appealed.

'Mr. Holmes has discovered evidence which is incontrovertible and it points to you, Mr. Carleton. Have you anything that can prove your innocence?' Lestrade said.

Carleton was silent for a long moment, then said, 'That is not evidence! Blood drops on a wall, wounds in a corpse! Why, it shall not be acceptable in any court.'

'You may be correct,' Holmes said. 'However, I believe a judge and jury *will* accept it, as did Lestrade and Scotland Yard, once I explain it to them.'

Carleton remained silent.

'We are waiting here with baited breath, for you to tell me where I have gone wrong,' Holmes stated.

'Well, it's all wrong!' Carleton blurted, then his keen mind evidently triggered on something and he smiled confidently, 'For one thing, neither you, nor Scotland Yard, have been able to produce Crosby. I'm afraid without that crucial person, Mr. Holmes, all your fanciful theories and make-believe evidence do not amount to a hill of beans.'

'Make-believe evidence!' I cried, enraged at the audacity of the fellow, but Holmes motioned me to silence.

Then for the first time I saw my friend's face fall as if he was unable to reply. His check had apparently been mated and we all knew it. Carleton saw his advantage and moved in for the *coup de grâce*.

'Mr. Holmes, you shall be hearing from my solicitor upon this matter presently, of that I can promise you,' Carleton said with tightly controlled anger. 'And you, Inspector Lestrade, I will see that you are put up on charges when I call in favours owed me by various of my political connections. I can promise you now that both of your careers have come to a much-deserved end. And, by the way, so has this interview. I want you all to leave these premises immediately!'

Roderick Carleton stood up then and pointed us to the exit of his library.

Sherlock Holmes slowly got out of his chair as if the weight of the world was upon his shoulders. At that moment I was despaired of my good friend. Could Carleton really destroy his career? And Lestrade's too? The man was a fiend. A killer of a woman and her children, he was surely capable of anything. Yes, he would most certainly do as much damage as possible through connections he had in high places. This had become a disaster.

It was a grim trio that walked slowly toward the doors of the library. We were defeated, leaving the killer, Carleton, boldly gloating as he watched us leave the room.

It was a terrible situation, Sherlock Holmes had failed! Now a killer, instead of being brought to book was going to escape justice completely.

I walked more quickly, eager to get out of that vile man's house. Holmes and Lestrade lagged behind me, the look of defeat etched upon their faces all too plainly. They walked more slowly, conversing in whispers. I could not bear to look at them and see their pain and despair. So I walked on ahead, to the front door where Carleton's butler with a smirk upon his face, held the door open for us to leave.

Suddenly my eyes were attracted by a rapid movement at the doorway outside the house. It was Constable Harris.

Harris quickly ran through the front door into the house, passing the butler and then saw me, 'Quick, where's Inspector Lestrade and Mr. Holmes!'

I pointed behind me to an alcove on the long hallway where they'd just left the library.

Harris ran over to them and all three men spoke for a long moment. I walked over but once I got there their discussion had broken up and Harris suddenly bolted outside the house again.

Lestrade and Holmes looked at me and they were now smiling. They immediately walked back into Carleton's library and I followed them.

Once Carleton saw us he barked, 'Didn't I order you to leave my home!'

Holmes and Lestrade just ignored his words and walked closer to Carleton, while I followed behind wondering just what was up now.

'This is outrageous!' the man shouted but there was less conviction behind his words when he saw Constable Harris now enter the library holding Toby on a leash.

Harris let the leash go and Toby rushed to the Great Detective who hugged and petted the huge bloodhound as it jumped up on its hind legs to greet my friend.

'Good dog, Toby! Well done!' Holmes said joyfully.

'What is the meaning of this?' Carleton ordered. 'Get that beast out of my house! All of you get out now!'

Holmes looked at Carleton and smiled broadly, enjoying the moment. 'You nearly had us. Of course, it all turned upon the fact that Crosby wasn't the killer of his family, but then you knew we had to find Crosby's body to prove that.'

Carleton stood by astonished at my companion's words.

Lestrade beamed now as Carleton's vaunted superiority and confidence seemed to slowly melt away before our eyes.

'Toby here, is a most talented canine,' Holmes began. 'Did you know he can smell out any scent I give him? You killed Crosby and took away his body after the murder. I knew you would hide the body, probably bury it, but where? Well, while Lestrade and I, with my friend, Doctor Watson, were confronting you with the evidence of your crimes — our own little bit of misdirection I might add — Lestrade's men with the assistance of Toby, were searching the grounds of your house for Crosby's body. Now they have found it.'

Constable Harris added, 'Mr. Holmes, Toby found Mr. Crosby's body wrapped in a bolt of cloth and buried on the grounds just as you said it would be. The corpse has two bullets in the chest. We also found the missing black leather valise and inside it was a pair of bloody gloves, bloody clothes, and a Webley revolver, recently fired. It was all in the grave with the corpse.'

Carleton's face fell then. I knew we had him for sure now.

Holmes explained, 'You had Crosby's body in your possession since the murder. When he was thought to be alive and in flight, it was assumed he could be anywhere in England or the Empire. His body posed no threat to you then.'

Carleton listened without saying a word.

'However,' my companion continued, 'once I was able to ascertain that Crosby was dead, and that you were the killer, it narrowed down his whereabouts considerably. Then I knew you had to have Crosby's body. There could be no other answer. All I had to do was determine where you had hidden it. I knew you would need to keep Crosby close. His body was the key to this entire mystery. You could ill afford to have that body ever found, or someone stumble upon it. That meant Crosby had to be here on the grounds somewhere. Probably buried. So Toby did his work while we kept you occupied.'

Carleton seemed to shrink before our eyes, but suddenly he pulled out a gun and aimed it at my friend, 'Well now, Mr. Holmes, you seem to have all the answers. Here's my answer. If I can not end your career one way, I can certainly end it by a bullet! Prepare to die, Mr. Sherlock Holmes!'

Carleton aimed his gun at my companion and I quickly withdrew my revolver from the pocket of my jacket. It had been resting in my hand ever since I'd come back into the room. I fired, as did Carleton. The two loud reports issued forth almost as one.

Carleton jumped when my bullet hit his arm, and that thankfully caused his aim to miss Holmes. The killer dropped the revolver and held his bleeding arm.

'Bravo, Watson!' Holmes shouted.

'Nice shooting, Doctor,' Lestrade smiled as he picked up Carleton's gun. Then he drew his own weapon to cover the prisoner, saying, 'Carleton, I am arresting you for the murder of the Crosby family.'

Lestrade took out a set of manacles that he handed to Harris who carefully placed them upon the prisoner, then the constable took the man away.

'Mr. Holmes!' Carleton pleaded in a high voice as he was taken from the room. 'I'll confess all, all I say, but keep me from the gallows! You made that offer to me! Mr. Holmes! Inspector Lestrade!'

Constable Harris took Carleton out of the room and none of us answered his pleas.

Lestrade nodded when the man was gone, 'He'll hang for sure and he deserves it.'

'When I remember what he did to that poor woman and her children . . . ' I said through clenched teeth.

'Quite right, Watson. A devil will soon get his due.'

⋆ ⋆ ⋆

Back at our rooms at Baker Street, Sherlock Holmes and I spent a well-deserved restful evening. First we enjoyed a delicious dinner compliments of our Mrs. Hudson, then a glass of after dinner port, and finally a good cigar, all topping off a most satisfying day and the conclusion of one of our most fascinating cases.

'He almost got away with it,' I said to my companion. 'What was it that gave the game away to you?'

Holmes smiled, 'Misdirection, Watson! Once I saw the particular configuration of blood splashes on the wall in the room where Mrs. Crosby had been stabbed, I suspected she had not been killed in the bed at all, but standing, up against the wall. The blood clusters there clearly indicated such. So I thought, why did the killer move the body and why place it in the bed?'

'Why, Holmes?' I asked.

'Cunning misdirection,' Holmes replied. 'It caused the police to miss the origin of the murder and thereby set them on the wrong tack from the beginning. Carleton also used a kitchen knife from the house for the crime, then left it behind as a further link to Crosby. More misdirection!' I nodded, following his logic.

Holmes continued, 'Once Toby found the blood in the library, that confirmed my suspicion Crosby had been murdered and it really set the case on its head.'

I nodded, remembering the various complexities.

'Watson, the world is full of obvious

things in which nobody by any chance ever observes. I believe there is much more we can learn from these methods.'

'Trifles,' I answered, rewarded by the smile that glowed across his face.

'Yes, those insignificant trifles,' Holmes replied. 'In fact, Watson, I believe that proper analysis of these blood patterns and sprayings at murder sites will some day open up an entirely new field of medical jurisprudence.'

'Well, Holmes, if not for you this case would have languished in obscurity with Crosby never being found and the true murderer never being brought to justice. It may have also proved the end of Lestrade's career, not to mention your own.'

Holmes nodded with a grin, 'Now, that would have been a pity.'

'Not to mention the fact that Carleton was going to shoot you dead,' I added sharply.

Holmes sighed, 'I do not fear death, my friend, only stagnation.'

'Well, I for one am glad that it is over.'

'Quite right, old boy.' Holmes said,

with a wink. 'This proved to be a case very much with a sanguinary solution.'

I nodded as my companion got up from his seat to pick up his beloved violin.

'Now, my friend, some soothing and gentle music to top off a most satisfactory evening.'

'Oh, no, Holmes ... not the violin again!'

MYCROFT'S GREAT GAME

I enter this account, for which I have been silent all these years, to set the record straight for posterity. I have instructed my solicitors to deliver it to my heirs and descendants 100 years after my death at a time when all principals involved will have long been deceased and unaffected by the facts herein.

It really was quite unfair, you know. My little brother Sherlock always getting all the credit. He had become quite the publicity hound lately, with Watson and Doyle positively fawning at his every word. Why, sometimes it is absolutely unbearable.

Oh, I know what you are thinking. I am Mycroft Holmes, solid, stodgy, overweight minion of the eccentric *Diogenes Club*, renowned recluse of Pall Mall, blah, blah, blah. Utter balderdash, I tell you!

While I had carefully fostered a veil of anonymity over my affairs and personage, there was much more to my work than anyone would have ever guessed. And while the official dispatches and the popular press positively fell over themselves to laud brother Sherlock's little accomplishments in his consulting detective 'hobby,' I performed my work in a totally unknown capacity, completely devoid of anyone's knowledge. My great powers and directives not even imagined by our politicians and the Fleet Street press, as I managed this vast worldwide enterprise of ours — the British Empire!

Now don't get me wrong — I dearly love my little brother, and it was hardly a matter at all for me to put up with his silly eccentricities and inconsistencies now and then, as I am sure he had so patiently put up with my own. It happens to the best of us, for we were true brothers, blood being thicker than water and all that sort of thing. Nevertheless, since our teen years we had gone our separate ways, and each in his own way, had achieved a measure of success.

I remember fondly when our guardian, Great Aunt Julia Vernet, had told young Sherlock and I on that summer day in the gazebo, 'I am sure that both my wonderful Holmes boys will go far in this world and make your marks, if you do not allow your great intellects to get the better of you. Promise me you will always remember to use your powers for only good purposes.'

We promised. We dearly loved Great Aunt Julia. She died not soon thereafter leaving us alone. It was a blow to Sherlock and I that we have never forgotten.

Ah, but that fond memory was from such a long time ago. From a much simpler world that was very far away from the present cold orb we are forced to inhabit today.

Today, it is 1891! We approach the dawn of a new century, an exciting modern age and a treacherous era of changing technology, international intrigue and dangerous nationalistic expansionism.

Now I must play the 'Great Game', doing my duty for the Empire I love. The Empire Great Aunt Julia so loved. Unlike brother Sherlock, I adhere to my Great Aunt's values. My brother feigns the vaunted Bohemian, but in reality, it was the very structures of Empire that allowed him to so indulge his activities in the criminal investigative arena.

Rather, it is I who bore the weight of Atlas upon my shoulders. It was the life I had chosen. I had no regrets. I had little choice then, for I was in too deep. It was, however, the one career I was eminently suited for. I had been very successful as well, but it had caused me to cut myself off from everyone and everything that might interfere with the performance of my duty. No one, not even my dear brother — especially *he* — had ever been allowed detailed knowledge of my work. It was best for Sherlock, best for myself, and best for the Empire I serve. Safer that way all around. For I was engaged in the most dangerous of games.

Now, I was aware that Sherlock has had some nebulous suspicion that I occasionally was involved in some kind of 'work' — for lack of a better word — for what we'll call 'the government'. He may have even suspected my influence reached to some at the highest levels. That was certainly true, but what of it?

Good Sherlock even fancied, in his most wildest dreams, to be sure, that I *was* the government. Of course I steadfastly denied everything. He had given that impression to Watson, and the good doctor had dutifully recorded such suppositions in his fictionalised accounts of my brother's cases. I knew Sherlock well and I thought this was nothing but a vain little conceit of his. He was too logical, far too observant, and I had made my plans too well in this venture. My overweight and sedentary life, the *Diogenes Club*, the 'recluse of Pall Mall' dodge, were all but elements of a clever ruse I incorporated into my overall airtight persona. I knew, in truth, Sherlock had no evidence of my business. Nothing. He may have said certain things for effect, and to Watson in general conversation, but he surely did not *believe* them. I intended to keep it that way.

The absolute truth was a lie I had weaved so well that logical Sherlock would never believe it. That truth was, that aside from the public figure-heads of our beloved Queen and noble PM — I was not merely some occasional influence in the government, but I was in fact, the Controlling Director behind the entire British Empire. There was a need for such a person. The Monarchy gave me their trust; politicians at the highest levels were able to effect a compromise. I was the natural choice. Actually, the 'Director-ship' merely broadened my existing powers and responsibilities. Thus was born the unofficial and very secret office of Controlling Director. From hidden vaults and rooms beneath the *Diogenes Club*, with a small group of dedicated specialists, I managed all that was the British Empire.

Certainly it was best that Sherlock did not know much of these matters. I hid it well; the facts of my activities have always eluded him. I was sure Sherlock's delicate sensibilities would cause us to be at loggerheads had he full knowledge of the import of my work and duties. I know he would have been upset by certain of my dealings. So I shielded Sherlock as best I could, even as I indulged him as he went his merry way on his criminal problems, as long as they did not conflict with my own plans. It was not always easy being Sherlock's smarter brother.

It is an axiom that in order for our government and Empire to succeed, certain of what I call 'prerequisites' must be realized and met. It is a sorry constant that occurs when one is involved in power politics — the Great Game, as it is sometimes called. However, I found myself constantly having to wander further afield to achieve objectives, often into hitherto unexplored and sometimes unsavoury areas to ensure success in my numerous ventures for the Empire. I am the first to admit that at times, I found it troubling. Such as this recent 'Moriarty affair'.

The basis of this problem began some years ago. In my position as Controlling Director of the Empire, it was I who allowed Moriarty and his minions to exist, and to some degree, even prosper. I knew it would be useful to the needs of the government and the Empire I served if my influence also extended into criminal society. So I made inroads into that sorry element. I discovered a most enterprising individual and realized that under the proper control, a criminal element could be most useful to our needs. I further realized that by having crime 'organized', it would better enable me to control it, thus being even more useful to my purposes. The criminal element contributes agents who readily perform the most unsavoury deeds that the regular military and most members of legitimate government agencies would never accept. So you see, in this cynical and dangerous game we play, they do have their uses.

And yet, I began to feel I had made an error in this chessboard of intrigue that I play upon our worldwide stage. Not all factors can always be considered, not all results so carefully manipulated. It began to disturb me to see Sherlock's obsession with Moriarty. While it was certainly well founded, it had been steadily growing. Now it threatened certain 'delicate situations' should Sherlock act too adroitly in this area, or if he found out too much information that was not within his preview to know and decided to act upon it.

My fear that this problem would come to a head was soon realized.

★　★　★

It was in the Spring of 1891, when Sherlock came to visit me at my Pall Mall lodgings. Thus began the narrative Watson was to record months later in his fictionalised account of the situation entitled, 'The Final Problem'. However, Doctor Watson's account would leave out certain important facts and replace them with my brother's own version. I shall remedy all that now, and tell the true story that has never been told.

Sherlock's visit to my rooms was certainly a surprise, to be sure. My brother and I led separate lives these many years and saw each other only occasionally. Now he entered my rooms quietly, thoughtful.

Sherlock looked worn and haggard but alert with the hunt. I knew he was in his element investigating some kind of criminal case, no doubt, and loving it. I knew this could be a difficult meeting for both of us.

After niceties had quickly been exchanged, in Sherlock's customary tart manner, we got down to the purpose of the meeting. He told me, once again, of his suspicions about Moriarty's activities. He asked if I knew anything about them. I gave some vague generalizations and once again denied knowledge of everything.

'Ah!' my brother said sharply, 'you know it is barely three years since the Ripper murders, Mycroft? The year 1888 is not long ago at all. You did not know anything about that matter either, then. I did not investigate the case, as you are well aware, though I was asked to do so by the official police.'

'So?' I said calmly, wondering where my dear brother was going with all this.

'Well, I did not investigate it . . . because I did not want to discover that it might be one of your 'little' projects.'

'That is outrageous!' I blew up in anger. I knew he was trying to provoke me. Inwardly I smiled at my brother's sharp boldness, but it did hurt. Once again, I denied everything.

He was silent, observing me closely, fingers steepled, thinking.

'Just what are you implying? That I killed those women, or had them murdered? You are so out of bounds on this, Sherlock, you have no idea!'

He said nothing.

'Well?' I asked sharply.

'Nothing. I did not come here to argue. Today three years later, there is Moriarty to consider,' he said. 'That is my one focus now.'

Here we were, back at Moriarty again. I felt his interest was bordering on obsession. I tried to dissuade him as best I could.

'I tell you, Sherlock, do not become overly involved in this Moriarty business. I do not advise you to travel to the Continent either,' I told him bluntly.

'My dear Mycroft,' he said with that glimmer of rich sarcasm in his cultured tones. He was being prissy with me. 'I would expect nothing less from one who detests travel and all modes of circumlocution to only embrace the sedentary life.'

'Nevertheless, Sherlock, you must be aware that it is a trap.'

'Of course,'

'And yet you persist?'

'And what is the alternative? Am I to forego an opportunity to smash

Moriarty and his organization once and for all!'

'Moriarty! Moriarty! You have the man on the brain! I tell you, in all truth, he is a rather small fish and of little consequence in the grand scheme of things,' I replied showing my annoyance.

Sherlock gave me a quizzical smile.

'No matter, Mycroft. I am off to the Continent.'

'To where?' I asked, incredulous.

'Why, to Meiringen, by way of Interlaken.'

'All the way to Switzerland?' I asked in obvious surprise. At least I showed him my surprise. He countered, likewise with a hint of astonishment. I could not help but smile.

'Indeed. I have a yen to see the Reichenbach Falls before I die.'

This kind of talk disturbed me and as Sherlock's brother I realized I had made a grievous error by allowing this situation to approach a crisis point. I knew something had to be done soon. I had already set my mind to working out a plan. Now I felt linked to this situation as if by handcuffs. When my brother left, little did any of us realize what actions would be set in motion and what momentous events would transpire.

Try as I might to dissuade Sherlock of his obsession, to be fair, his assumptions about Moriarty's activities were more often correct than not. Moriarty certainly was an unsavoury sort. However, not all that had been attributed to Moriarty, nor even the worst of it, by dear brother Sherlock, had been at Moriarty's cause or design. Some of it had been at my own. Which was the crux of the matter between us that I needed to keep from my brother at all costs. This information, what I tend to call 'Empire business' — and the less said on those matters the better — must forever be kept from Sherlock. For my brother to find out the truth, could destroy our friendship forever.

★   ★   ★

I grew concerned that events were swirling out of hand when no sooner did

Sherlock leave my Pall Mall lodgings that evening to visit his good friend Doctor Watson, and I settle down to what I thought would be a relaxing evening repose, than I had a surprise visitor.

Tall, thin, wiry and furtive, he looked like some human manifestation of a ferret on the prowl, or some mongoose from the Indian sub-continent ready to devour a poisonous python. With his hunched back and bald pate, deep-set eyes that did not miss much at all, I knew the man instantly as he strode the 22 steps to my outer door, knocked once lightly, and was admitted by Burbage, my squire and retainer.

Professor James Moriarty stood in the doorway as I motioned him quickly inside. Sherlock's supposed 'Napoleon of Crime', indeed! He was a nervous and fearful little man who knew he was breaking a dire rule in our relationship by ever approaching me directly in public or private — all our communications being done clandestinely through third and fourth parties.

I nodded, 'Take a seat, if you please. Tell me what is on your mind.'

'I will stand. I will be brief.'

'Continue,' I said firmly, my substantial girth made him seem to dwindle before me. He knew this was a dangerous breach contacting me directly — a serious breaking of the rules — but it was for an important reason, so we 'got to the point', as the Americans are so fond of doing.

Moriarty sighed, 'It is becoming impossible! Impossible, I tell you! Your brother is at me all the time now. The harassment, the constant investigating of my affairs. What have I ever done to interfere with him or his friends, Watson and Doyle? Why does he persecute me?'

I did not say anything for the moment. It was a serious matter to see this man so upset. He was no one to trifle with.

Moriarty continued, 'I tell you Mr. Holmes, I am at my wits end with this affair. Call off your brother or I shall have no choice in the matter. I do not want to act, but know this; I will never stand in the dock. I will not allow your brother to be the cause of my loss of liberty. I have stayed my hand these past months out of respect for our mutual interests. I can not do so forever.'

I nodded slowly; Sherlock had certainly muddled up this affair royally.

'You spoke to my brother?' I asked Moriarty.

'Yes, and he will not see reason. Why, he actually drew a revolver and kept it handy as we spoke. I was highly insulted by that gesture.'

I nodded, I could imagine the scene.

Moriarty continued, 'I do not wish to interfere with our business arrangements, they have been beneficial and lucrative, so I come to you now, pleading Mr. Holmes, before things get out of hand or someone makes a terrible mistake that we shall all regret.'

The subtle threat in Moriarty's words was all too evident.

'The mistake, my good Professor, would be if any harm ever came to my brother. I hope you understand that completely,' I said, my eyes burning into his own.

He looked away, nodded slowly.

'Then we are in agreement on that

matter, at least?' I asked, emphasizing my previous warning with all seriousness.

'Yes. No harm shall befall him, but please, this is quite out of hand now and becoming dangerous. I have come to you for advice and assistance.'

'And you shall have it, Professor,' I replied, more upbeat now that he was evidently willing to seek a non-violent solution to the problem.

'So then, instruct me. What shall I do?' Moriarty asked.

'Nothing, Professor. You will do nothing.'

Moriarty looked at me curiously.

'I will explain.'

'Please do.'

I was silent, thoughtful. Finally I had it all worked out.

'My brother is going on a little trip to Switzerland, hiking in the Interlaken area, perhaps even a visit to the majestic Reichenbach Falls? Are you familiar with the region?' I asked Moriarty.

He fidgeted, still standing before me, still refusing the seat I had offered him. He said, 'I am. My knowledge and influence extends to the Continent, just as yours does. But what is the significance of your brother's travel there?'

'Ah, that is the interesting matter. Through various agencies, I have made it appear that you are in fact, 'after Sherlock'; that you intend to remove him once and for all.'

'Anticipating my future move?' Moriarty smiled, then thought better of it.

'A move you shall *not* be making, but yes, to your question,' I said, adding, 'Your little visit to him the other day has certainly played into brother Sherlock's fascination with your affairs. I have also been concerned because I have noticed a conflict growing between the two of you for some time.'

'Not on my part, I can assure you,' Moriarty asserted.

I nodded, 'That may be true. Regardless, I have begun the manufacture of a scenario that will make my brother decide to leave London. Fleeing to the Continent, he believes your agents will attempt to hound him to an early demise. He will, of course sense a trap, and in doing so, quickly reverse it to trap you instead.'

Moriarty's smile melted. He stood careful, waiting.

'Of course, nothing could be further from the truth,' I added.

Moriarty nodded, but he looked surprised, confused. He said, 'But I thought . . . '

'Absolutely, and that is the beauty of the plan. Sherlock will flee London in the belief that he is being chased by you and your minions. Meanwhile you will remain in London.'

Moriarty smiled ferret-like, asked, 'That will remove your brother's meddling from my affairs?'

'Yes, you will be free of him, and you and your organization will remain in London to perform your work for me once again, uninterrupted,' I added.

'Then your brother will be sent on a wild goose chase?' Moriarty said with a grin.

'He needs the rest, a nice hike in the Alps shall do him good. Don't you think? I have set it up where Watson will accompany him,' I added.

'I am still concerned that he plans a

confrontation of some kind.'

I smiled, 'He absolutely does. But nothing of the kind shall occur. Since you will be safely ensconced in London, that confrontation cannot possibly take place. You see, I know my brother Sherlock's mind too well. He may fantasise about some titanic struggle abroad, perhaps even at the Falls of the Reichenbach. The opportunities for melodramatic heroics, I am sure, will not be lost on Sherlock. But it will be a non-event. Instead, Sherlock will be traipsing abroad, safe and out of your hair, and you shall be safe in London, unhampered, and never the twain shall meet.'

Moriarty nodded, 'I am satisfied. I appreciate your assistance in the nullification of this danger to my person.'

'That is just as well, Professor. Now you may rest easy. By tomorrow, Sherlock and Watson will begin their grand tour, and you shall be free and unencumbered once again. We will work out details in the coming months and I shall convince Sherlock to drop the matter before he returns.'

'I thank you, Mr. Holmes. I knew that coming to you with this problem was the appropriate way to attain satisfaction.'

★   ★   ★

Burbage let Professor Moriarty out and carefully closed the door behind him. We were alone now.

I looked to my aide. Burbage was as taciturn as ever, his lips sealed tight, but I felt the thoughts going round in his head. Alexander Burbage, late of the Indian Army, marksman, secret agent, Afghani scout, and now my manservant, confidential secretary, bodyguard, and sometimes man-of-action.

'Well?' I asked, I could see he was fairly bursting to speak his mind but would never do so unless I prompted him.

'I fear your brother will never leave London,' he said matter-of-factly.

'He will certainly think seriously about it after you set fire to his rooms at 221B later tonight!' I said.

'I, set fire to his rooms? Are you serious?'

'Oh, absolutely, but Watson and he will not be there, of course. And it will be — after all, a very minor fire that will do no real damage — it will look far worse than it actually is. You can manage that, can you not? I shall instruct you later. It will, of course, be blamed on Moriarty and his 'gang' — all part of my plan to pressure my dear brother to leave London.'

'But I was here when he visited you earlier today. I am sure I heard him tell you that he already planned to leave London for the Continent,' Burbage replied, confused now.

'Aye, Burbage, you heard correctly,' I said carefully. 'So Sherlock would have me *believe*. In fact, that was all a ruse. You see, Sherlock has suspicions about my place and work, but no hard facts. Our little association on the Affair of the Naval Treaty notwithstanding did not begin to display the length and extent of my interests. So he tempts me with a plan where he proposes to do exactly what I would like him to do. And I, playing his game, dutifully reply with all earnestness, that I do not like the idea at all. I further state the obvious, that he is desperately needed here in London. Now would be the worst possible time for him to leave. And he knows it. For truth to tell, we have each noticed that it tends to cause an unnatural excitement in the criminal classes when Sherlock is not in the city.'

Burbage shook his head as if to clear the cobwebs of gamesmanship. He was a man of action, not used to the intellectual double thinking and conundrums required when chess pieces are moved in this Great Game of ours.

'Now let me see if I understand this,' he said finally. 'Sherlock feigns a trip to the Continent, though he has no actual intent of going. He says this all just to gain your attention and see your reaction. Meanwhile, you do not give him satisfaction, instead you react in the reverse of what you actually want and intend. Which is the reverse of what Sherlock believes that you want. It seems like the reverse of logic to me. My poor head hurts from the thought of it all!'

I laughed, 'You have it absolutely! And

there you see the beauty. For as you are perplexed, imagine poor Sherlock! I will gently prod my little brother into accepting the validity of his initial idea — that a trip to the Continent is just what he needs now. He will come to the realization that London is too hot to hold him. That is why I had you perform several highly convincing but absolutely unsuccessful attempts upon his life recently — obviously the work of this dread 'Moriarty gang'. Sherlock will leave London convinced that the gang is hot on his trail and will seek a confrontation on the Continent. He will set a trap for Moriarty at Reichenbach. He believes that then he will solve the Moriarty problem once and for all. One way or another.'

'Aye, and in the meantime, he will be out of London and out of your hair,' Burbage said with a smile.

'Yes. You see I dearly love my brother, but I do not take Moriarty lightly, and my brother will not drop the matter. That places him in dire peril. While Moriarty is a useful agent, I have no illusions about this situation. Sherlock has enmeshed himself in a serious game. When a dangerous man is in fear of his liberty, unless something is done to remedy that situation, panic cannot be far behind. And during panic, a man will lash out and perform actions that may not be in his best interest. Moriarty values our alliance, but he values his freedom more and Sherlock is trimming his sails appreciably. Lately my brother has been stepping up his efforts to destroy the entire Moriarty organisation. That put each man in danger from the other. An unacceptable situation. A remedy was needed. Now I can never countenance any attack by Moriarty on my dear brother. Nor Sherlock doing anything against our vital interests with Moriarty. Both men must remain safe and allowed to continue to operate. Therefore, my plan. As things stand now, this appears to be an acceptable solution to protect both men and at the same time continue my business with Moriarty. As you know, his people have become most useful lately in ferreting out and exposing anarchists and agent provocateurs who seek to throw our nation into socialist revolution. Through their efforts we have uncovered three bomb plots and broken up two cells of saboteurs and spies, all dutifully handled without police or press interference.'

★　★　★

The next morning I was at the hansom cab stand that Watson frequented. I was the driver of the third rig, suitably disguised. That talent runs in the Holmes family, as Sherlock often makes use of it in his investigations, and Watson chronicles the same in his little detection stories. I knew Sherlock would instruct Watson to pass the first and second cab and take the third one. I smiled to myself as I saw the good doctor approach.

'Aye, Guv, where to?' I barked in an indistinguishable cockney growl. Now I ask you, good reader, had I been the entirely sedentary and reclusive creature I was made out to be, would I had been a part of such activity? Would I had even been capable of doing such a thing? Truth to tell, I often acted as my own agent in certain delicate matters such as this.

'Victoria Station, my good man, if you please,' Watson said, getting in the cab. 'There's an extra guinea in it for you if you make all haste and follow my directions.' Then he sat back quiet, thoughtful. He hardly noticed me at all, his attention concentrated on possible watchers and followers. And while he was in absolutely no danger, I'm sure he felt as if danger was surrounding him and following his every move. I was careful to remember that my brother had certainly instructed Watson to carry his old service revolver. So I had to act with care as I knew my passenger was quite nervous and must be armed.

I climbed down and loaded the good doctor's trunks and baggage. All loaded up, with a grunt I gave the old mare a taste of the stick and we were off.

I've always enjoyed a brisk ride through the London streets at dawn but actually driving the cab was a real thrill for me. I get away so infrequently these days that donning a disguise and fooling poor old

Watson so handily was a bit of a lark. I even played gruff conversation with him, until he barked at me, 'Please! Just drive the cab!' Then muttering to himself, 'The man simply does not know his place!'

I smiled to myself. On Watson's part, I could see the concern and worry in his face as he tried to sit silently in the back seat, thinking dark thoughts of what the next few days might bring. I felt for him then, but realized that my deceit was protecting Sherlock and him from danger. I knew he would approve, if only for the safely of my brother, his good friend.

Of course, Watson supposed as did Sherlock, that Moriarty and his henchmen were hotly after them at that very moment. The fire last night in the rooms at 221B had shocked Sherlock, as I knew it would. Burbage's work had certainly done the trick. This morning both men were hurrying out of London to catch the boat-train to the Continent. I sighed and allowed myself a satisfied grin as I drove the cab quickly through the empty London streets. I had averted a possible fatal confrontation between my brother and Moriarty. I was quite satisfied with the matter at the present time.

After I deposited Watson at Victoria Station, I watched with some amusement as he went about the place as inconspicuous as possible — or as inconspicuous as possible for good Watson — frightfully amusing, let me tell you. From a safe distance, still in my disguise, I watched when Sherlock and Watson finally boarded the 7AM Express to the coast. When the train pulled out, I waited to be sure that my brother did not perform one of his little 'double-back' tricks. When I was sure no one had left the train, I drove off, back to Pall Mall. I was happy that my brother and Watson were now on their way to the Continent. Out of London, safe from Moriarty.

Being Sherlock's smarter brother sometimes leads me to a slight overconfidence in our relationship and my talents. Even, I dare say, an uncommon arrogance on my part. That was to prove my undoing, as well as events from a hitherto unforeseen source by the name of Colonel Sebastian Moran. Little did I realize that all my fine underhanded plans would crash down upon my head before I knew it.

★ ★ ★

The next morning Burbage woke me early with alarming news. Moriarty was still in London as we agreed, but he had secretly sent his most trusted man, Colonel Sebastian Moran, to follow my brother and Watson. Moriarty had sent a note saying it was 'just a simple precaution to be sure my brother does not return to London'. However, Moriarty's 'simple precaution' now upset the apple cart and had thrown all my plans into disarray. For I knew that once Sherlock discovered he was being followed — and he surely would — he would seek the very confrontation I had worked so hard to avoid.

'That maniac with an air-gun is stalking my brother!' I fairly shouted at Burbage. 'He's Moriarty's chief hench-man. He is not a member of the gang, so our people did not watch him like the others. Moriarty keeps him on separate status for use in delicate and special cases. Now he has slipped away. This is an outrage, Alex. Very bad!'

My man, Alex Burbage, nodded grimly, 'I can be ready to leave within the hour, sir.'

I looked up at Alex. 'It will be dangerous. While I thought I could reason with Moriarty — after all, this was all in his own self-interest — Moran is altogether something different. He is a killer. If he gets it in his mind, he will kill whoever is in his way — Sherlock, Watson, or you — and Moriarty's restrictions on him be damned!'

Burbage smiled, said, 'A little travel, the prospect of action, it sounds like fun. I will leave immediately, sir.'

'Thank you, Alex. Good man!' I said, touched by his loyalty and willingness to help. We shook hands, I said, 'Be careful, Alex. Follow Sherlock and Watson, make no contact, just observe and report back to me via coded telegram each evening. And keep a sharp eye on Moran! He's a bad one, and while ostensibly under the thumb of our professor friend not to take violent action, he likes to freelance too much for his own good. Keep me informed.'

★ ★ ★

Burbage was a good man. I felt entirely confident with him on the case. His talents in combat and with weapons were superior to Moran's. His loyalty was unquestioned. He was just the man for the job, my eyes and ears in this matter on the Continent.

The first report from Burbage was brought to me next evening on a silver salver where I sat reading the *Times* in my chair at the *Diogenes Club*.

Without a word, Wilson placed the salver down upon my reading table and then quietly departed. I saw a folded piece of foolscap that had been sent upstairs to me from the secret offices below by my chief of Intelligence, Captain Hargrove. Already deciphered, I opened the paper and read Burbage's first telegraphed report carefully.

It read:

M. HAVE REACHED YOUR BROTHER
AND W STOP ALL APPEARS WELL STOP
NO SIGN OF M STOP TOMORROW
INTERLAKEN AND FALLS STOP WILL
REPORT NEXT EVENING STOP AB

That was the last time I heard from Alexander Burbage. By the next evening when there had been no report from him I became concerned. The next day I dispatched two agents from Special Branch to follow him. Two days later their report, pieced together with Doctor Watson's added comments, formed the picture of what really transpired on that foggy morning at the Reichenbach Falls.

My brother always expected that someone would be following him. Had my original plan gone into effect unhampered, all would have been fine. There would have been no pursuit. Sherlock would have been perplexed, but finding no evidence of anyone tracking him, he would have been relegated to nothing more sinister than a harmless tourist. Moran changed all that by his very presence. Whether he meant my brother harm or not, whether he was stalking with murderous intent or just to observe, neither I nor Sherlock could have known for certain. Unfortunately, while Moran stalked Sherlock, he also set himself up as bait. So as Moran watched my brother, my man Burbage watched both of them. It was not long before wily Sherlock doubled-back on his tracks and soon stood to confront Colonel Sebastian Moran on the heights over the Reichenbach.

A terrible fight ensued.

Watson told me later that he was on his way back from the hotel, where he had been called away on a medical emergency. A subterfuge by Moran to get Watson out of the picture, with my brother's obvious compliance to protect his friend. But good Watson realized the trick and raced back just in time to see two figures locked in a death struggle at the height of the fog enshrouded Falls. Watson could see my brother plainly fighting for his life against a man whom he took for Moriarty. The thick fog obscured what happened next. Suddenly, out of the swirling mist a body hurled downward to the roiling waters below. Watson gasped. Was it Sherlock? Was it Moriarty?

Watson frantically raced to where he had seen the body land. It appeared the man had fallen into the turbulent river, badly injured, he had made his way to the shore only to die. Watson ran over to the man, naturally fearing it was Sherlock. He frantically turned the man over, face-up, surprised to gaze upon a face that he did not know at all.

Sherlock then came out of the shrubbery and Watson surprised and relieved, let out a shout of joy.

'Holmes! You're alive!'

'Indeed, Watson, though there are those who would be disappointed with that fact.'

'What happened?' Watson had asked.

Sherlock said nothing as he went over to examine the body.

Both were surprised the man was still alive, though barely. Watson did what he could, but it was obvious without serious medical attention the man would soon be dead.

Sherlock said, 'Good Burbage, you saved my life. I don't know how to thank you.'

'You know the man, Holmes?' Watson had asked.

It was, of course, Burbage. He had also seen the fight but was far closer and stepped in to save Sherlock's life. It was Burbage who Moran had caused to drop off the Falls as he made his escape.

'Yes, Watson. I sense my brother Mycroft's involvement here.'

'Mycroft?'

Sherlock nodded grimly, then to the injured man, 'Tell me, Burbage, what were you doing here?'

Burbage coughed, tried to steady his gaze, 'Moriarty betrayed your brother, sent Moran. I had to stop him.'

Moriarty betrayed Mycroft? Naturally Sherlock thought the answer odd and so he questioned Burbage further.

Burbage, dying, sick with delirium and in great pain told Sherlock all he knew about the plan to cause him to leave London. Sherlock was obviously upset by this deceit on my part, but what my man said next actually enraged him. For before Burbage died, he babbled a long detailed account of the alliance between myself and Moriarty and of some of our common projects. When Burbage died, Watson told me the look on Sherlock's face appeared as if he had died as well. The look of pained betrayal was hard set in his eyes and it was terrible to see.

Watson told me that when Sherlock first heard this news, he could see my brother's face turn ashen and Sherlock shouted my name in rage. Sherlock had lost control and was furious. 'I have been betrayed, Watson!' he shouted angrily. 'Not only is my brother allied with the same forces that I have risked my life to fight, dedicated my profession to destroy, but it is now obvious that he has been working with them all along. This is just too much!'

Of course, not being there to give Sherlock my side of the story, I was at a considerable disadvantage. But Sherlock would not have listened anyway.

Watson told me later, 'I have never seen your brother so upset. It was most unlike him. He had lost all composure and even commented that not even the cocaine needle could assuage his pain this time. He actually used profanity in conjunction with your name. He said he was finished with you, London and the Empire and that he would never come back.'

I was shattered by this news. Sherlock now knew I had not only used Moriarty on certain matters, but that some of the 'Napoleon of Crime''s activities were in fact, attributed to *me!* That would be an affront I knew my brother could never accept. I feared his reaction, for I knew it would be extreme.

'Then,' Watson continued, 'your brother gave me instructions on what I must do and say about this matter before he told me goodbye.'

'What did he say?' I asked Watson.

'As far as anyone knows, Sherlock Holmes met his death at the Reichenbach. This is the last case I shall write. I am to write no more of his cases for publication in the popular press,' Watson said, adding, 'He told me he will travel the globe, see the pyramids, perhaps seek an audience or studies with the Dali Lama.'

I harrumphed my displeasure. Of course it was utter nonsense.

Watson shrugged, 'I tried to convince Sherlock to return but upon his death, Burbage told your brother such information that caused him great anger and distress.'

Indeed! Sherlock finding out that some of the actions taken by Moriarty, had in fact, been at my direction and design was the one thing I feared the most. I was crushed. *I* was the reason Sherlock was never coming back to London. It was because *I* was in London! I grew despondent and morose.

Watson shook his head sadly, added, 'Aside from Moriarty and Moran, you and I are the only ones who know that Sherlock is still alive. I haven't even told Doyle the truth. He never liked your brother anyway.'

I nodded, there was nothing to do about it now. Once Sherlock had made up his mind it was set in stone. I had damaged his pride, but far worse, I had betrayed him. Even if it was for his own good, I had deceived him and now he knows the worst of it. My involvement with Moriarty. It was terrible!

Watson, afterwards began to write his last Sherlock Holmes story for the *Strand*, as directed by my brother, calling it 'The Final Problem' — ending with Sherlock's death at the Reichenbach at the hands of Moriarty. And that, as Sherlock told Watson before he came home to London, was the end of that!

I made the prerequisite funds available to Mrs. Hudson to keep up the rooms at 221B. I hoped Sherlock would be back some day, once he dropped this silly notion of anger at what I had done. After all, everything I had done was for his protection and England's. Well, most of it, at any rate. As time went by though, I began to realize how wrong I had been.

I used my agents from time to time to carry cash and letters of explanation to my brother. His travels seemed varied and eclectic. His use of the name 'Sigerson', claiming to be a Norwegian explorer, did not put me off his track. Wily Sherlock kept the money but always returned the letters to my agents unread. He made it clear to me it was over between us.

But it was not over for me. Since that day the rift between Sherlock and I weighed heavily upon me. I wanted to mend that break at any cost and bring Sherlock back to London. So from that day on, I worked on a plan with Watson that I hoped would set everything right.

★　★　★

It had been three years now since Sherlock had left and I do miss him. Though we were always separated, there was always a connection that resonated between us. Two great intellects. The last two Holmes brothers left alive. It was a shame it had come to this.

In the meantime I continued my work for the Empire. It was a struggle, but rewarding in its own way. The Empire was now at its height and my work progressed well. Over the last months, through my various agents, including Moriarty's organization, there had been many successes.

I had managed to defuse one revolution, end two minor wars, begin one invasion, annex new territory, free a dozen hostages, cause distress among the French, confound the Germans, foster an alliance with the Czar, succeed in three assassinations and prevent two others. This string of successes ended with the murder of young Ronald Adair in London on March 30, 1894.

Much had been made of the murder of this young dilettante and scion of the lesser nobility in the popular press, but would it shock you to know that he was one of my most able agents?

His tragic murder by Colonel Sebestian Moran, up to his dirty tricks once again, had been doubly troublesome for me, for it precipitated what I had feared most in recent months, conflict between Moriarty's gang and my own Special Branch people.

It seemed that without Sherlock in London, the criminal classes — and the organised criminals in particular, of which Professor Moriarty had lately achieved an impressive consolidation of control — were making their own play for power. I began to realize I had created a monster. It is times like these that I especially miss the services of my brother and men like Burbage. I felt more alone than ever.

★ ★ ★

It was early April when virtual warfare between our two organizations broke out. My operatives in the Special Branch called it 'The Silent War'. There were serious political problems, probably instigated by Moriarty, and they took my full attention so that I did not notice the connection with his other actions. We missed some telling clues early on, all beneath the vision of the press and the police. So very British. I really must compliment Moriarty. It began with an inconsequential fall, then an accident by hansom cab, a heart aliment, later there was a suicide or a lovers quarrel gone bad. Before we knew what was happening we had lost half a dozen prime operatives and I found myself under siege.

Now I dare not even return to my lodgings across the street at Pall Mall. Should I do so and some attempt be made upon my person that is successful or causes some public spectacle, it would cause undue questions, which cannot be allowed. Thus I cannot leave the confines of the *Diogenes Club*. So long as I remain in this secure bastion, I am safe from Moriarty and his minions. The sad irony of this situation is not lost on me. My brother's attempt to destroy Moriarty and his entire organization three years ago had been the correct thing to do. I should never have stopped him. Sherlock always understood the criminal mind far better than I. He knew there was no reasoning with such people. I knew then it was time to cut my ties with Moriarty for good altogether.

The situation had become serious when I heard from Doctor Watson. I had not seen him since that day he had come back from the Continent after my brother had let out on his travels. Watson told me the most astounding and welcome news; Sherlock was back in London! The Adair murder had called him back, for Sherlock realized the meaning of such a bold move and the danger that it placed me in. It was an alarm to us that Moriarty was making his move. Watson said that my brother was back to help me and that he wanted to meet with me later at his rooms at 221B.

'That's wonderful news!' I told Watson. 'This is a perfect time for us to start our plan. Leak a message of this meeting so Moriarty is sure to find out. I will do the rest.'

I must admit that the prospect of seeing Sherlock again and our reconciliation did much to improve my spirits and I eagerly looked forward to our meeting later that evening. I knew leaving the confines of the club could be dangerous, but I took precautions. I had Hargrove see to it that Lestrade sent over two of his best men from Scotland Yard to accompany me.

★   ★   ★

All was going well until we turned onto Baker Street and I realized the two plainclothes police were in the employ of Moriarty. Though in disguise, and their papers had all been quite correct — their reputation had preceded them. I finally recognized them as Scottish specialists in murder, Jamison and Conner. This, I am afraid was not what I had planned, but by then it was too late. They had a weapon on me and I had no choice but to allow them to bring me to the destination where I knew I was to be assassinated. It was the empty house across from 221B. The very house my brother Sherlock used for some of his more clandestine activities.

I was brought into the house, and taken upstairs at gunpoint.

'Aye, Guv, someone of great importance wants to see you. On the upper floor,' Connor said prodding me up the steps. His partner, Jamison, following behind quietly.

When I reached the top of the stairs I was confronted by the sinister figure of Professor James Moriarty.

'Welcome, Mr. Holmes. It is so good to see you could actually bring yourself to leave the protection of your club to join us here tonight. It has been a number of years since our last meeting. At that time I seem to remember there were numerous issues left unresolved. I believe I can promise you that they shall all be settled this evening.'

'Where is my brother?' I asked defiantly.

Moriarty smiled, 'How sad. The vaunted reunion of the Holmes Brothers finally after so many years. There will be no meeting, but you shall see your brother presently, I assure you.'

His dark words put a dread feeling upon me. I began to realize that Moriarty had a far more sinister plan in mind than just my own murder.

'What have you done to him? You'll hang for this, Professor!' I growled.

Moriarty nodded, motioning his men to gag me and bring me forward into the next room. There I saw Colonel Sebastian Moran at the front window with a rifle in a sniper stance. He was aiming his notorious air gun at a figure silhouetted in the window across the street from us. I was alarmed, more so when I realized that the window was the front room of the top apartment at 221B Baker Street and the figure silhouetted in the centre window was that of my brother, Sherlock.

'Tonight, Mr. Holmes, I clean up all loose ends in this affair. It has been a long road for us to get to this point. Beginning with your meddlesome brother, Sherlock. He eluded Colonel Moran at the Falls. He'll not get away this time.'

I watched the silhouette of my brother in the window across the street, wishing that he would get up and move safely out of range. I saw him move slightly, turn his head a bit, but he still presented a full shot for Moran's murderous weapon.

I wanted to shout out to Sherlock in warning, but the gun pressed tightly in my back by Conner and the gag stuffed in my mouth by Jamison made it impossible. Moriarty's men held me firmly. So I just stood there watching with dreadful fear. Here I had come to meet Sherlock and there he was, waiting for me patiently, and I would never see him again. I felt like crying and then I saw Moran take aim. Moriarty rubbed his hands together in anticipation.

Moriarty said, 'Colonel Moran, you may fire when ready.'

Moran smiled, savouring the bloody moment, said, 'Yes, Professor.' Then he slowly squeezed off a shot. There was a slight whoosh, and a moment later I saw a tiny explosion in the centre of the silhouette of my brother's head.

Moran put down his weapon, stood up and said proudly, 'Sherlock Holmes is dead finally, once and for all, Professor.'

My heart sank. A tear streamed down my cheek. My brother dead? It was inconceivable. Terrible! I cried, knowing I would soon join him in death. That was the reunion Moriarty had planned for us.

'Good,' Moriarty said, satisfied, then added, 'Sherlock's brother, Mycroft, will soon join him.'

'Not so fast, Professor Moriarty!' A voice boomed from the doorway at the other end of the room. It was my brother, Sherlock, standing tall and bold, and beside him was good old Watson, Inspector Lestrade and a host of armed

Scotland Yard detectives.

The trap was sprung and the rats were left with no place to hide now.

The men from Scotland Yard were upon Jamison and Conner immediately. They were disarmed, put in irons and taken away.

Lestrade commented, 'A pretty pair, those two, wanted for murder throughout the High Country. It'll be the assizes for them soon enough in Edinburgh.'

Moran, seeing the way the wind was blowing raised his hands in surrender. Lestrade's men took him into custody and held him.

Moriarty, enraged at the sudden reversal of his fortunes quickly drew a knife and came at me before anyone could act. He held me in an iron grip with the blade to my neck. 'I'll slit his throat if you don't all back off!' he ordered.

Everyone held back, waiting, fearing the worst.

Sherlock calmly said, 'Let me have your revolver, please, Watson.'

I saw Watson put the weapon in my brother's hand.

Sherlock cocked the hammer back, even as I could feel Moriarty's knife tickle the folds of flesh at my throat. This had *not* been in my plan for the events of the evening.

I saw Sherlock take careful aim.

Everyone was frozen, waiting to see what would happen next.

Moriarty barked at Sherlock, 'I will certainly kill your brother if you do not drop your weapon and stand back!'

I watched fascinated as Sherlock held his arm out steady and straight, extended with Watson's revolver aimed at Moriarty's head.

'Drop the knife, Professor. It is over. Harm Mycroft and you will not live to hang,' Sherlock said sternly.

The face-off was incredible, the tension in the room, electric. Everyone held their breath.

Moriarty lowered the knife. He was an intelligent man, surely common sense was to prevail. I could feel the blade move away from my throat. I let out a breath of profound relief, and then I saw what was in Moriarty's eyes. The hatred that was there shocked me. It was like looking into his soul and it was ugly. Repulsive. The gag still prevented me from talking, but with my eyes I implored Sherlock to shoot. Could Sherlock see that Moriarty wanted us all to believe he was coming to reason, that he would soon surrender? All the time he was planning to slit my throat in one quick gesture, then hurl his knife into Sherlock's chest as soon as he saw the opportunity. Moriarty lowered the knife further . . .

Sherlock did not buy the bait. He did not lower his weapon. He did not waver.

Moriarty saw all was lost. He quickly moved his arm upward bringing the knife back to my throat for the killing blow.

One loud report issued from the revolver in Sherlock's hand!

The explosion was ear shattering and terrible.

Moriarty froze as did everyone in the room.

I tried to move, to get away.

Moriarty still held me tightly. I remember thinking, had Sherlock missed? It was inconceivable, but . . .

Then Morarity's arm continued upward once again, the blade of his knife touching my throat. I remember feeling the coldness of the steel, seeing Sherlock and Watson's terrified faces. Why did not Sherlock take another shot? What had happened?

Then suddenly the knife left Moriarty's hand to fall and clatter on the floor, and his hold on me loosened and fell away. I turned and saw his surprised face; the coldness of his reptilian eyes as the fire in those eyes seemed to dissolve before me. His great criminal intellect melting away in death as I watched. There was a tiny hole in the centre of his forehead and drops of blood now began suddenly pouring down his face. Then Moriarty collapsed to the floor dead, and I sighed with relief as Sherlock and Watson ran to my side.

'Good shot, Sherlock!' I said, once I had taken the gag out of my mouth and regained my composure somewhat. 'You saved my life. Thank you.'

'You mean to tell me this was not a part of yours and Watson's plan?' he said with a smile.

I shrugged, 'Indeed, however, I am relieved that you were able to improvise a correction so handily. But how did you know I had been taken hostage?'

'Good Watson here kept an eye on you after he gave you the news of our meeting. He alerted me to the fact that Moriarty's men had abducted you. I confess, I expected some such action from our enemy. The one thing you can count on in any plan no matter how well formulated, is that something will always go wrong. The criminal mind is a dark and devious morass but it functions at a rather primordial level. So accordingly, I made my own plan, and here we are!'

'I thought Moran had murdered you,' I said. 'I saw your head, the silhouette moved, so I thought . . .'

'Aye, and so did Moran, and that's what convinced him and Moriarty. It was a pretty set-up, Moriarty literally champing at the bit at the prospect of murdering both Holmes brothers in the same evening when they were so close to meeting and reconciling their differences. It was a master plan, worthy of the Napoleon of Crime.'

I nodded, 'Indeed, it was an evil plan. I will never understand the criminal mind as you do. I am just relieved we are all safe and have concluded this Moriarty business once and for all.'

At that moment, Moran was dragged past us by two stout Bobbies. He shouted, 'Why? Why am I being arrested? I did not kill Sherlock Holmes! He is alive and here!'

Lestrade held up his hand. Then Sherlock brought over the air gun and gave it to Lestrade, saying, 'Here Inspector, I believe this rather unique gun will test positive as the weapon used in the murder of the Honourable Ronald Adair.'

'Aye, Holmes,' Lestrade said, 'I'm sure that it will.'

'And, Inspector,' I added, 'that should be quite enough evidence to send Colonel Moran to the gallows. He has eluded the hangman for far too long.'

Lestrade nodded, 'So it will, Mr. Holmes, eh, Mr. Mycroft Holmes.'

Sherlock and I smiled.

Moran struggled and shouted threats.

Lestrade barked to his men, 'Get him out of here!'

Sherlock and I joined Watson as he preformed the final examination on the body of the late Professor James Moriarty.

'Official cause of death,' Watson said, getting up from the corpse, 'one bullet in the head. Death was almost instantaneous.' Then to the waiting Bobbies, 'You men can take the body away now.'

Sherlock, Watson and I sat in the rooms at 221B across the street a short time later.

'I see you had Mrs. Hudson keep our rooms just as they were. I thank you, Mycroft.'

'It was the least I could do,' I said.

Sherlock nodded, 'It certainly was. Especially after you had your man Burbage set fire to them!'

'Now, Sherlock . . . ' I said carefully, 'It was really, after all, a very minor fire.'

Sherlock laughed, 'Fear not, older brother, my anger is gone and I know that in your own way, you tried to protect me, even as you protected your own interests.'

'It seemed the best course open at the time,' I replied.

'And anyway, we have a celebration! Watson, break out that bottle of Napoleon Brandy you have kept for a special occasion. For there can be no occasion more special than this one — the end of Moriarty and the liberation of the world from his grasp — and we have a bonus! The capture and future hanging of Colonel Moran . . .'

'Not to mention you saved my life, Sherlock,' I added.

'Quite right, Mycroft. Glad to be of service. You and Watson had a good plan, the use of both Holmes brothers as bait could not fail to bring out Moriarty and Moran where we could finally get at them. Your mistake was failing to realize that no plan, no matter how brilliant, is a solid item. It is fluid, always open to change and amendment. You saw a chance to bring out our enemies, they saw an opportunity to twist your plan against you. However, they neglected to factor in my own action. So the wax bust to mark me as an easy target as I waited to meet you in these very rooms. It was a situation I knew Moriarty could not resist. And while our enemies concentrated on the image in this window, Watson, Lestrade and I, with a triple brace of good London Bobbies were quietly entering the house from the backyard.'

'Mrs. Hudson helped,' Watson added, pouring brandy and passing it out. 'She bravely stayed in here moving the wax bust of Sherlock to trick Moran and not make him suspicious.'

'Good Mrs. Hudson,' Sherlock said gently sipping his brandy.

'When Moriarty thought you were dead', I said to Sherlock, 'he became confident. Even I noticed how he grew lax and did not post a guard, and that is how you were able to move up the stairs undetected. It was the perfect time to make your move,' I added. 'But even you did not know he would take me hostage with a knife to my throat?'

'Why, Mycroft, you continually surprise me! Actually I did. But the game was up for him no matter what and he knew it.

He wanted me dead, not you. He could not get at me with a knife and I had Watson's revolver and knew how to use it. He gave me no choice, so I fired. Your eyes told me what I must do.'

I nodded, it was all becoming clear to me know and I gained new respect for my little brother and his great talents.

'But I did not think you had it in you, Mycroft, lowering yourself to actual ratiocination, this uncommon interest in the criminal mind bodes well for you,' Sherlock told me with a laugh and a gleam in his eye. 'Why, I believe, I'll make a detective of you yet.'

'Your acid wit has returned, I see,' I said a bit testily.

'It never left, brother,' Sherlock replied sternly.

'Well, I think it is time I return to my club, there are matters that need my direct attention,' I said.

'Indeed,' Sherlock said tartly. 'Are you already thinking of a replacement for Moriarty?'

I sighed. I had no anger left in me. 'No, Sherlock, that is over. I am truly sorry for deceiving you. These last three years have made me realize much and I hope that the rift I have opened between us can now be mended. I will go back to the club, tidy up a few matters, confer with Captain Hargrove, and then tender my resignation. I believe retirement is in order and frankly, I look forward to it now.'

Sherlock was surprised but pleased. He came over to me and shook my hand, saying, 'Mycroft, you did what you thought best. A man, no man, should be chastised for that. I know Great Aunt Julia would have been proud of you for all you have done over the years. I am proud of you for what you did today and for what you just said.'

A tear came to my eye then and I saw it mirrored in Sherlock's own eyes.

Sherlock wrapped his arms around me and we hugged each other silently for one brief endless moment as Watson watched in wonder.

'You know, I too think I shall retire, some day, Mycroft. Perhaps to the Sussex Downs and a study of bee culture? It can be most fascinating.'

'Is that wise, Holmes?' Watson interjected with evident concern as my brother and I both looked at him and smiled.

'With Moriarty and Moran gone,' Sherlock answered contritely, 'I am afraid that London's criminal element will be reduced to the banal and the inept. Lestrade will be well within his depth, I am sure.'

Watson and I nodded, knowing all too well of my brother's opinion of the official police.

'However, Mycroft,' Sherlock added seriously, 'while I am the first to admit that your 'work' has been a serious bone of contention between us for years, with your retirement I fear the Empire has lost its most successful advocate and protector. Know this, our vaunted 'Pax Britannia' exists in no small part due to your tireless work and effort. That is a considerable accomplishment, even if it can never be made public. With you gone from the scene, the politicians will be in charge again and God alone knows what horrors they'll perpetuate upon the body politic. For instance, I see ugly war brewing in

South Africa among the Boers in years to come. I see a tragedy coming our way there. But far worse, without your direction of our ship of state, I fear within 20 short years we will find ourselves engaged in a world-wide conflagration the likes of which this planet has never seen before.'

I nodded, 'I am aware of the projections.'

'Then you know the politicians will only expand the length and depth of the misery and carnage,' Sherlock added.

'Yes, brother, I know that and it saddens me, for I have worked for the Empire all my life and I do not want to see the approaching sunset. Nevertheless, the Empire is changing, and so too the world, and we must all change with it. Or be left behind. It is time for me to move on, and for you ... to study bees in Sussex? Indeed!'

I took another sip of Watson's excellent brandy.

'Well, Watson, surely this has been a case worthy of your efforts for the popular press?' Sherlock said.

'Yes, I would like your permission to

write it up for the *Strand*.'

'Indeed, certainly, but with certain restrictions. Of course all mention of my brother and his 'government' service must be deleted. I'm afraid you will have to leave Moriarty out of the story as well. Knowledge of his surviving Reichenbach will not only contradict your previously published narrative of this case, making you look rather foolish, but it will cause fear and chaos in the criminal underground and among the public. Moran can easily fit the bill of your villain, and he is the actual murderer of young Adair. But Watson, do not publish the story for at least 10 years. I see 1904 as an adequate date for the appearance to the public of such a tale. What do you think?' Sherlock asked.

'Of course, I shall abide by your wishes,' Watson replied.

'Good. Thank you, old friend. I rather like the thought of being dead, at least where the public and popular press are concerned. And it certainly will surprise the criminal element who believe that I am no more, when I appear and confront them with their crimes,' Sherlock added with a grin.

I nodded, 'It sounds like it would make an interesting case, Doctor. I shall look forward to reading it in the *Strand* . . . some day.'

'Hah! Ably put, Mycroft!' Sherlock said, 'And who knows, between now and then — two Holmes brothers, retired, on our own and left to our devices — why we may even join forces on occasion when a particularly complex or interesting problem may arise, eh, Mycroft?'

I smiled at my brother, 'I don't see why not, Sherlock *Holmes & Holmes*, Consultants. It does have a certain ring to it, don't you think?'

We do hope that you have enjoyed reading this large print book.

Did you know that all of our titles are available for purchase?

We publish a wide range of high quality large print books including:
Romances, Mysteries, Classics
General Fiction
Non Fiction and Westerns

Special interest titles available in large print are:
The Little Oxford Dictionary
Music Book, Song Book
Hymn Book, Service Book

Also available from us courtesy of Oxford University Press:
Young Readers' Dictionary
(large print edition)
Young Readers' Thesaurus
(large print edition)

For further information or a free brochure, please contact us at:
Ulverscroft Large Print Books Ltd.,
The Green, Bradgate Road, Anstey,
Leicester, LE7 7FU, England.
Tel: (00 44) **0116 236 4325**
Fax: (00 44) **0116 234 0205**

THE FREEDOM ARMY

E. C. Tubb

To escape war, humanity takes a drug that kills emotion. But insurgents, including the returning astronauts from a mission to Mars, refuse to take the drug and wage an armed rebellion. The Freedom Army, which includes the Physicist Burges, is beseiged in a bunker. However, Burges constructs a gateway to another dimension — an alternate existence — and ex space pilot Lanson leads their escape . . . only to face an alternate world where humanity is enslaved by a toad-like alien race, the Zytlen!

THE SPIKED BOY

John Russell Fearn

Dick Palmer and Will Snell are great friends, both former highwaymen who were subsequently exonerated. However, they become fugitives from the law again when members of a mysterious gang of murderers and kidnappers use their names to frame them. Then when the gang kidnap Palmer's wife the two friends are plunged into a deadly struggle to rescue her. But they are up against an evil and secret organization — and the sadistic Simon Pendexter, who swings a 'spiked boy' . . .

HELL IS EMPTY

J. F. Straker

On a lonely island in a Scottish loch, Donald Grant and his self-willed wife Kay are staying with his aunt and uncle, and their daughter Janet. Three desperate men, looking for a hideout, have also come to the island: Bull, Fred and Joe, are gunmen on the run from a robbery, and filled with seething mistrust for one another. Now the island community faces fear and violence in a situation that will lead to tragedy . . .

SKYBORNE SAPPER

David Bingley

World War II. Young Nick Burrows is embittered with himself, and society. Hoping to meet his brother Harry, he volunteers for the paratroops, but the brothers miss each other and Nick throws himself into the fighting in Tunisia with the First Army. When Nick is in action he's different — men trust him. His scheming keeps them alive in the events after the first parachute drop. When Nick finally meets Harry, he realises that he has 'found himself' at last.

JOURNEY INTO TERROR

E. C. Tubb

The first exploratory expedition to Pluto returns with the Captain, Jules Carmodine, alone . . . What happened to the crew remains a mystery as Carmodine is suffering from amnesia, and mentally and physically broken in health. Later, although his health improves, the amnesia remains. Then, when Carmodine is forced to return to Pluto, he faces a journey into terror. He must remember what happened on that first mission — otherwise the second expedition will suffer exactly the same fate as the first . . .